SURRENDERED VIII

By

Peggy Patrick

ISBN-13: 978-09962959-7-0

Cover Design by Charlene Raddon
http:/cover-ops.blogspot.com

Special thank you to my sweet friend Jackie Gary for your reading, editing, insight and support. My appreciation of you, Jackie, is immeasurable.

And always and forever to my daughter, Lisa Patrick Sandmann. I could not have made this Surrendered journey without your boundless patience and hard work and generous humor! Thank you! Love you!

SURRENDERED VIII

CHAPTER ONE

Hank Walton had always been one to take things in stride, at least by outward appearances. He didn't react too quickly to good or bad news—but simply and slowly moved to deal with whatever a situation called for.

Right now, sitting in the office of a doctor of internal medicine, he figured he would have broken that calm, cool trait long about five minutes ago and lost all control. But—somehow his insides were about as peaceful as they'd ever been. Maybe more so.

Dr. Devon leaned back in his swivel chair behind his desk and stared at the folders that were stacked neatly on the right corner of it. He'd just told a kind, older gentleman that his life could end any moment because he had a blood clot in his shoulder—the reason his arm was swelled and touchy. The sonogram was clear. He'd seen such clots as these many times in his thirty years of medicine and they were almost always fatal—especially as big as Mr. Walton's. He desperately wanted to give the man some hope, even if it wouldn't last long.

"Hank…I would like for you to stay in the hospital tonight and let me give you something intravenously to try and dissolve it."

Hank looked at him, searching the doc's eyes for—something. Truth? A ray of hope? "What are my chances if I do that?"

"Fifty-fifty," he lied. "Better than leaving here and doing nothing."

After a full minute— "Okay. I need to make a phone call first."

"I'll make arrangements for you. You're welcome to use my office, my phone…whatever you need."

"Thank you."

The doctor left and Hank blew out a long breath he didn't know he was holding. *Lord Almighty!* This was the last thing he expected this day to hand him. It was very possible that he'd never lay eyes on High Point Dude Ranch again. Never return home to his sassy little wife, Martha. Who was going to cook for all those dudes and the ranch hands? The cabins and teepees were all full. This was supposed to be a simple doctor appointment for a badly bruised arm, get a pill and go home. He'd come here at Martha's insistence. She had made the appointment for him and threatened him with his own egg spatula early this morning.

He felt his calm, placid nervous system trying to switch gears. He'd never been faced so point blank with his own mortality. Oh, he knew someday he would die—but realizing that *someday* could be today—or tomorrow—was unnerving. He wasn't ready. Martha needed him. And that passel of kids out there of Jesse's and Donny's and Beau's and all the rest—they needed Grandpa Hank.

He stood and picked up the receiver of the desk phone. He'd better call Jesse.

Jesse Brandon walked out of his home office at High Point and headed down the hallway toward the kitchen. To say he walked slow, feeling like he was dragging two boots full of concrete might be understating his steps.

It was an hour away from supper and no less than thirty people to feed—dudes and ranch hands combined. Hank Walton had cooked and served chuck wagon meals for High Point for many years, never missing a day—but he hadn't made it back from his doctor's appointment.

His wife Laura and Granny Martha Walton were jumping hoops in the ranch kitchen getting large pots of mac and cheese, pinto beans, fried chicken legs and he wasn't sure what all—ready to carry out to the chuck wagon and serve the evening meal. And sometime in the middle of all this chatter and activity, he had to deliver some devastating news—Grandpa Hank wasn't going to make it in time to help serve. He possibly wasn't coming home at all.

A few minutes earlier, he'd stuck his head inside the kitchen door from the patio to check on the food situation when Laura asked him to run check phone messages. She hadn't been able to stop and answer the last several calls. Hank had left a message with a call back number that turned out to be his doctor's personal cell phone. And now, after a short conversation with a Dr. Devon, he was headed back into the kitchen to change some lives with the worst possible news.

Jesse stopped short of entering the kitchen and prayed. A lot of people outside would be gathering to be fed, but this news couldn't wait. *Lord, show me how to handle this.*

After a few long moments—he turned around suddenly and headed outside through the front door of the house. *What would I do without You, Lord, as my counselor?*

He found Beau Vance in the barn along with his brother, Donny Brandon, grooming and feeding the horses that had carried dudes on the afternoon trail ride. The look on Jesse's face caused them both to stop and stare at him.

"I need you both to finish up with that as quick as you can."

He told them what the doctor said about Hank's condition. "Beau, ride out and tell AJ Call to drop what he's doing and come to the house here. Get Mitch Corry and the two of you need to take over the chuck wagon duties. Food's all in the kitchen. Bring it out—serve it up—entertain our guests the best you can. If Daisy Corry or your wife, Carly, is available, tell them they'll go on payroll today if they can help with the guests.

"Yes, sir. We can handle it." Beau tightened the cinch on the one horse still saddled, mounted up and left without looking back. He headed for the canyon where he knew Mitch would be with a few kids on a hayride.

AJ worked for Judd Luke on the neighboring Double OO Ranch, but he should be here at High Point this afternoon, out on the north side repairing a section of fence for Jesse.

"Donny," Jesse continued tying up loose ends, "my kids are at your house with Reeny. Let them know where we will be and that I'll call them later."

"I'll see that they're taken care of for you."

Jesse went back around to the front of the house to the office and called the Double OO to let Judd and Toni Luke know the situation. Judd was pastor of the Cowboy Church that Laura's son, Andy Parker, had built on property that joined High Point. His dad, Matthew Parker, was killed in a car wreck when Andy was barely four years old and had secretly purchased this property next to his boyhood friend, Jesse Brandon's ranch.

Laura had been opposed to moving from her secure city life to the country, so Matthew left the charge to his best friend to see that Andy received that property in the event of his death.

Jesse and Laura soon fell in love and raised Andy at High Point where he now lives with his young wife Summer and her two girls—Emma Jo and Rachel Logan.

Jesse entered the kitchen where a flurry of activity blocked out much notice of him. He saw that the stove was turned off as he walked over and took Laura's hand and then Granny Martha's to command both of their attention. He knew the best way to do this was to just come out with it.

"Ladies, I have some…bad news. Hank was admitted to the hospital after he saw the doctor today. They found a large blood clot in his shoulder. They're giving him some medicine to try to dissolve it, so…we need to head on up there to be with him."

Both women stared at him as if waiting for the punch line to a joke.

Finally, Martha spoke with an even and calm tone, "But, they don't expect the meds to work, do they?"

"He's in trouble with this thing, Martha. Get ready to go. I've got help on the way to take care of the evening meal."

Both women laid down spoons and dish towels—untied their aprons without a word and headed for the back door. Before reaching the dually, Laura said, "The kids are up at Reeny's. I have to tell them."

"Donny already headed up to do that."

AJ rode into the yard then and dismounted before his horse fully stopped. "Jesse, what's the problem?"

"Hank. He's in Jackson Hospital. Doesn't sound good, AJ. You need to come on up soon as you can. I've got to get Martha up there."

"I'll be right behind you." He led his horse toward the barn where his truck was parked.

AJ Call and Hank had hired on to the Double OO and High Point, respectively, close to the same time and had struck up a friendship that now spanned close to a couple of decades. Jesse knew Hank would draw some comfort from AJ being there.

The Brandons and Granny Martha entered Hank's room where an IV was dripping—Jesse and Laura stood back close to the door to allow Martha a private greeting.

As she approached the bed, Hank stretched both arms toward her and she reached for him, then laid her head on his chest. They both began to cry and talk at the same time, holding on, literally, for dear life.

Jesse couldn't hold up after that scene. He backed out and walked away, stopping in front of the wall of windows at the end of a hallway. He'd been too busy to allow himself to think about what was happening. The doctor told him to notify Hank's family because he didn't expect him to live through this. Jesse believed Hank had no blood relatives. He had revealed to him that he had been in the witness protection program for many years after shooting and killing a Mafia kingpin's son. Hank Walton was a police officer with another name in another life. But every man, woman, child, horse and dog on both High Point and the Double OO ranches were Hank's family. There were a lot of us and we all needed him. Jesse let tears run down his face unchecked. Sometimes a man just needs to cry.

After a while he walked back to Hank's room. Laura was gone, but AJ was standing with Martha. When Jesse went to the opposite side of the bed, he realized they'd given Hank a sedative. He was very drowsy, but not asleep.

"Hey, cowboy,"—Jesse grasped his hand and Hank closed his fingers tightly around his friend's— "You've got friends up here praying for you. Just remember that God is a whole lot bigger than some old blood clot."

"Thank you. I'll remember." He slurred his words through a half grin—then he closed his eyes and seemed to be asleep, his breathing short and even.

He glanced around surprised that the room had filled up—Donny and Reeny, Judd and Toni Luke, their daughter, Jenny and Les and Kaitlyn Kane.

A nurse wound her way through the crowded room, then craned her neck around to scan the faces.

"Maybe some of us should go back out," Donny said to her.

"No, please stay. I was just thinking that Mr. Walton must be a very important man."

Jesse looked at her. "You have no idea, mam—no idea how important he is to this bunch."

She smiled and nodded. "I just need to check his blood pressure and you all should stay as long as you like."

After the nurse left, Martha laid her arm across his middle and her head on his chest. She began to pat him on his side, raised up and kissed his chest, then lay her head back down. "You know I need you, Hank Walton," she whispered, but it was loud enough that everybody heard.

They all began to file out into the hallway, some swiping at their eyes. AJ stayed with Martha a couple more minutes before giving her and Hank their privacy. Just as he walked out into the hall, the entire group had gathered in a tight circle with arms around each other. Jesse made a space for him and pulled him into the group.

Judd Luke prayed in broken sentences, unable to hold back his emotions. He asked for God's Perfect Will for Hank—but made known his request, as the Bible says to do. *"So, Lord, we all are asking You, if You can do without our Hank for a while longer—we would like to keep him here. That's our request of You, according to Your Word. You also said that we have not because we ask not—so we're asking this in the Name of Jesus Christ. Thank you, Lord. Amen.*"

There wasn't a dry eye in the prayer circle nor in the lineup of several nurses and other hospital personnel who had grasped hands behind the circle and prayed with them.

Jesse stepped back inside far enough to see that Martha hadn't moved from her embrace, then he headed toward the front area of the building where he'd seen the hospital chapel. He felt that's where he'd find his wife.

Pulling off his hat, he slowly pushed the door open and stepped inside. It was dark with the exception of a few glowing candles, but he could see her clearly. Laura was on her knees in front of the alter, leaning forward with her face close to the floor. He knew his wife was a dedicated prayer warrior—up in the middle of the night praying—but he'd never witnessed her this way.

He quietly sat down on the back pew just inside the door and began to silently pray. He believed that if this was Hank's call to go home to Heaven, they could pray till their hair fell out and it wouldn't change a thing. But, just the same, this is what you do in a crisis—pray. And just as Pastor Judd had told God in his prayer a minute ago— *You said to come make our requests known to You.* So, he continued to pray, listing all the reasons he could think of as to why Hank needed to stay on the earth longer. With his reasons prayed, he sat quietly and waited for his beautiful bride of nearly twenty-three years to get up off the floor.

After a couple minutes passed, the chapel door opened slowly and quietly. Donny stepped inside and Jesse stood.

"Something's happening to Hank, Jesse. His breathing... is rough and..." he choked up and couldn't say more.

Jesse grabbed his emotions, swallowing hard. He had to be strong for the others. "The clot's moving." He turned to look at Laura just as she got on her feet and joined them.

"This is not unto death. It's over now," she said calmly. Her face was tear-streaked but coated with the glowing Peace of God.

The men looked at each other, then back at her.

"I saw it explode," she whispered.

The brothers didn't understand but said nothing. The three of them walked silently back to Hank's room where everyone except Martha and AJ were lined up against the wall in the hallway. Inside the room was a flurry of activity with nurses and doctors moving in and out.

Jesse, Laura and Donny went inside where they could catch glimpses of Hank. Martha was draped across him as though trying to physically hold him here as a couple of nurses simply moved around her with tubes and a lab tray.

AJ stepped over to the Brandons and told them, "He suddenly started mumbling something like—*It's not unto death...* and then he couldn't hardly catch a breath. His heart was beating really fast."

The Brandon brothers looked at Laura then. "Honey, that's what *you* said in the chapel."

She nodded. "That's what God said to me while I was praying, then I saw a huge explosion in a vision."

Jesse walked up toward the head of the bed where he could see Hank better. He was awake and didn't seem to be too distressed. He put a hand on Hank's shoulder, "You've got about twenty-five people gathered outside your door, old friend—most of the ranch is here and a herd of church folks from town. This hospital thinks they've got a famous person in here."

Hank lifted sleepy eyes up to see Jesse and attempted to smile. "Wh...what...blew up?" He mumbled at a bare whisper.

"What blew up?" Jesse repeated. "Well, you had a little episode of some kind, but I think you're doing all right now."

Laura heard the exchange and immediately stepped up beside her husband. "Hank, did you see something explode in here?"

He nodded and his eyes became frantic with fear.

"Hank, do you remember that you have a blood clot in your arm?"

"Yes," he whispered.

"I saw a vision a few minutes ago of a tremendous explosion. Millions of tiny particles blew everywhere. Apparently, we both saw the same thing."

He nodded, "Yes."

"I believe God touched that clot and we saw it disintegrate and go away."

Dr. Devon had heard the exchange between Laura and his patient and abruptly, loudly exclaimed, "You definitely had an embolism, Mr. Walton. We just don't know where it went."

The room quickly cleared of all medical staff, then Hank feebly reached for Martha's hand. She grasped it with both her hands. He looked from Jesse to Laura and said, "Get Judd."

Without hesitation Jesse nodded and turned to go. "We'll get him." He, Laura, and Donny headed out of the room. AJ followed.

Jesse addressed the crowd, "Folks, Hank had an embolism. That's what they expected to happen. He's all right for now. Doctor's not sure where the thing went, but it appears we might have a miracle man in our midst."

A hoot and some gasps rippled down the hall.

"Right now, he's asking for you, Pastor Judd."

Judd went in and around to the far side of the bed. Hank looked pale, like he'd been through a terrible ordeal. But there was something else in his eyes that went deeper than the physical.

"How ya doing, buddy?"

"Pray. I don't…know how…to say it." Hank could only whisper, but those eyes were pleading out loud.

"I'd be honored to pray with you, Hank. Is there something besides getting you well that you want to pray about?"

He nodded, his eyes boring into Judd's. "Me…to be saved."

Judd realized Hank was afraid. He was scared of dying. "Hank, I've known you a long time. You've been to my church for years. I believe you are a saved man…ready for Heaven whenever your time comes."

He shook his head. "No…I…don't know if I am. Pray."

Judd nodded agreement and lay his hand over Hank's. "I'll pray and you repeat my words."

He nodded as Martha lay her hand on top of Judd's with tears streaming down her face.

"Dear Lord, I know I'm a sinner. Forgive me."

Hank whispered the words and immediately began to cry.

"I believe Jesus died for me and rose again. I ask You, Jesus, to be my Savior and my Lord. Thank You, Jesus, for saving me. Amen.

Hank sobbed through the words and at the end, he added, *"I'm sorry, God. I don't blame You anymore."* His sobs were coming from the heart of a broken, repentant man.

Judd didn't know his story—what he had blamed God for, but he did know that the woman standing beside him, crying with him and nodding her head knew. He squeezed Hank and Martha's hands and went out before he lost it. He swallowed hard but the lump in his throat didn't want to budge.

Jesse followed him a short way down the hall. "Everything okay?"

He nodded and brushed the back of his hand across his eyes. "Hank was blaming God for something. He needed to clear the air with Him. Whoo…that was tough."

Jesse patted his shoulder and left him to get control of his emotions. He knew it was about the tragic death of Hank's parents. Hank confided the story to him several years ago.

Buck Rhea was Hank's real name—A rookie cop who drove up on a Mafia drug exchange and ended up taking a bullet, but not before he shot and killed a drug lord's son. Buck's parents were targeted for revenge and murdered in their rural modest farmhouse—the murderers vowing that Buck Rhea was next. His parents were buried before he even knew about it and he immediately entered the witness protection program and became Hank Walton.

The pain and torment of guilt that Jesse knew Hank must have experienced all these many years, hurt Jesse's heart for him. But tonight, he was relieved at the choice *Buck Rhea* had just made —to turn loose of his anger at God over his parent's violent deaths. The day he left the hospital, he was flown out of state with a new identity—not even allowed to visit his mother and dad's graves. Not to this day.

That remembrance struck a nerve in his mind—his eyes widening at the idea forming in his head. Grandpa Hank and Granny Martha needed a vacation—a trip to California—after all these decades. If he survives this ordeal, and it sounded like God had heard their many prayers, he would personally escort the two of them to visit the resting place of Henry and Jill Rhea.

Les Kane opened the screen door to the mud room at the back of his log house that had served him as foreman's headquarters for the Double OO Ranch for the past twenty years. He set his mud and manure splattered boots just inside and stepped on the thick red throw rug with his sock feet. He always tried to be careful with the outdoor mess he brought inside from his workday.

Kaitlyn was an immaculate housekeeper, but not once in their seventeen years of marriage could he remember her ever getting crossways over the dirt in the laundry or the shower.

She had heard her husband's dually come in and slid the garlic bread into the oven. His favorite Ritz cracker chicken casserole was bubbly hot. By the time the individual bowls of salad and quart jar drinking glasses of sweet tea was on the bar, which served as their dining table, he entered the kitchen.

Les was slightly over six-foot-tall in his sock feet—lean and muscled with wide brown eyes that she had never tired of looking into after nearly two decades. Les Kane was *cowboy,* through and through; a rugged and hard-driving man out on the range, but as meek and gentle as a lamb as soon as he entered the presence of the one love of his life—his *missus*—as he often called her.

"Smells like my missus is a woman after my heart. Is that a Ritz chicken I smell?" He sniffed the air with emphasis. "And garlic?" He placed his hand over his heart. "My cup runneth over, my lady."

He had thoroughly brushed his dusty clothes off at the barn and washed his hands, arms and face before getting into his truck to drive home. He was comfortable with stepping up and wrapping her in his arms. Her arms went around his neck and they held each other tightly without a word for a long few second. Then he kissed her and smacked his lips. A deep shaky breath involuntarily sucked into his lungs and they both laughed.

She poked a finger into his chest, "We better sit down and eat before I wind up throwing you down right here in the kitchen floor."

He laughed aloud. "Now…little lady…I might have to consider foregoing that mouthwatering chicken that you…"

"Sit!"

"Yes, mam." He straddled his bar stool and glanced around the kitchen. "I don't see de-sert," he quipped.

With her back to him, she pulled the pan of bread out of the top oven. "Oh, don't you worry, mister. I've got *de-sert,*" she mocked his slang.

"And don't I know it!" he mumbled, then took a long swig of sweet tea.

Kaitlyn had been through a lot of heartache for one young woman. It had been a full twenty years since the first time he'd laid eyes on her sexy little self. His mind flashed back to the day, as a young veterinarian, he'd carelessly dropped a glob of horse wormer in the barn alleyway of her folks' barn. Their beloved old dog licked it up and died in front of him and Kaitlyn. He and Katy were engaged to be married at that time—until that unforgivable act destroyed the whole family. Her younger brother had died, causing her mom to drive away in inconsolable grief and was never heard from again. Her dad took to his bed and died—leaving Kaitlyn Grace alone—and pregnant. Les was the father, but he'd left town in a storm of anger and heartache—never knowing about the pregnancy—and left her to experience the loss of their baby boy alone.

After they'd found each other again, Les vowed to her and before God Almighty, that he'd spend every day there after loving her like there would be no tomorrow. That alone proved to be the easiest thing he's ever done in his life. The only tough part was their inability to conceive again.

After seventeen years, they both settled into a mindset that baby Danny would be their only child. They quietly celebrated his birthday every year, asking God to relay their love to him on that day.

They finished their supper with small talk about the day. Then, she cleaned the kitchen while he showered.

Just as she turned the kitchen lights out, he strode in wearing gray sweats and a black, short-sleeved T-shirt—hands on his hips and an exaggerated frown on his face.

"Hey, where's my *de-sert* you promised?"

She smiled and winked, then headed for the bedroom. "Follow me."

Seriously? Now he was more than all for a roll in the sack—and he'd *never* say so—but he really had his mouth set on some pie or puddin'—or heck, a cookie. He followed her.

After quickly changing her lounge dress for a simple pink silk nightgown, she pulled a large cloth off a big lump in the corner of the room, unveiling a bucket of ice containing a bottle of champagne. Two glasses waited on her bedside lamp table.

"Wow—what's the occasion?" His brain was stripping its gears trying to think. *Birthday? Anniversary? What did I forget?*

"If you'll pour us each a glass, I'll get a couple slices of your favorite New York cheesecake."

Oh, Lord help me here—I *know* I forgot something. *When's our anniversary?* He couldn't think. He knew he'd been busy—early morning to late evenings. What got past him? He decided the best course of action would be to keep his mouth shut and pour the champagne.

The bed pillows were all fluffed up to prop up on, as they sometimes did to drink coffee in the mornings, so he set a fizzing glass on each of their lamp tables while she did the same with two small plates of cheesecake.

After they were propped up in their King-sized log bed that had been their favorite spot on the ranch for the past seventeen years—they sipped their bubbly and indulged in their favorite pie.

"You never did answer my question."

"Oh…you mean the occasion question?"

He chuckled. "Yeah, that one."

I could tell you, but maybe you should just read it."

"*Read* it?"

They both set their dishes on their tables and she pulled a folded newspaper from her lamp table drawer. He noticed she held the paper like it was a fragile piece of fine china as she laid it on his lap. Her hands were shaking, bringing a concerned crease in his brow.

"Are we celebrating something that's in this newspaper?"

She nodded slightly and said nothing.

He stared at her for several seconds, then slowly opened the thick fold of the paper. It was right there on the page. He stared hard, his heart picking up speed. He knew without touching it what it would say. All he could do was continue staring at the oblong stick that lay between the folds of the Jackson Weekly. It was a pregnancy test.

Tears welled instantly as his eyes reddened and he didn't try to hide them. Gently he picked it up and read the clear, dark lettering on the test—*Pregnant.*

"My God—Katie." He put an arm around her back and pulled her against him as his other hand caressed her teary-wet face. His own tears trickled into the top of her hair.

They had hoped and prayed for this for so long but had lost hope after almost two decades.

He moved his hand down and laid his palm like a whisper on her flat stomach. "A baby—Our baby's in there. Oh, sweet Jesus. Have…you seen a doctor?"

"Yes. I went a couple days ago. They verified that my own test was right."

"So, everything's all right, then?"

"Well…yes…" her voice trailed off.

"What does that mean?"

"Only that I'm forty years old and this pregnancy is considered high risk. That only means I'll have to be checked out more often than normal until the baby comes."

Worry coated his face. "Katie, you have single handedly made my entire life worthwhile. You are going to have to settle for being next to bedridden until this is over…you can't take any chances trying to work or…"

"Les, honey, do you remember how you and I finally got together?"

He stared off into space for a moment, then nodded his head slowly as he looked back at her and planted a quick kiss on her forehead. "Do you mean when God had to *literally* speak a bone of my bone and flesh of my flesh lesson to both of us? I'll never forget that."

"Yes, and neither will I. He let both of us know without a doubt that it was His Will for us to be together." She patted his hand that lay protectively across her abdomen. "And we need to remember—that same God has this baby in His capable Hands."

They both were silent for a minute. "I think we should pray right now and ask Him to take care of you and this baby." Les wrapped her up in his arms and prayed.

After a few minutes of laying entwined in each other's arms, he got up and locked up the house for the night. It hadn't occurred to him that he was closing in on fifty years old—Kaitlyn forty.

He stood in the middle of the dark house and whispered, "Thank You, Jesus," then made his way back to Katie's side, to the very spot where this blessing was given to them.

***

CHAPTER TWO

"Drake...Ben...either of you seen Hank Walton this afternoon?"

Both stopped in the middle of unsaddling horses inside the barn and turned around to look at Donny Brandon. They shook their heads after glancing at each other.

"Is there a problem," Ben asked?

Donny lifted his Stetson off his head far enough to scratch an itchy spot, then settled it back on. "I don't think so. He seems to have moved away from Granny Martha's radar screen. She's about a nine and a half on the conniption scale."

All three chuckled.

Drake Henson reached up and dragged the saddle off the trail horse he was untacking for the day. "Do we need to hunt him up, Mr. Brandon?"

"Naw...he's not far. He'll show up. Thanks." Donny left.

Drake was a new hire at High Point when Hank Walton had his blood clot episode. That was six weeks ago. That's when he learned just how close knit this Brandon bunch was with family and their ranch hands. At first, he didn't know how to react to all the kindness and religious stuff these people exhibited. He hadn't known much of either where he came from in the southwest. He was raised in a saddle on a New Mexico ranch by a father who had nothing to say to him unless it was to curse at him or use a leather strap on him. He never knew half the time what the whippings were for and the other half was because he'd missed his calf with his loop or let a horse throw him. The only good thing he could see from those eight years was that it took one savagely rank horse to unseat him and his roping skills were far better than average.

Drake was an only child. His parents divorced when he was barely out of diapers. His mother died in a car wreck when he was ten and his dad came and picked him up the day of her funeral. He'd never been allowed to grieve for his mom. Tears for any reason would ensure a whipping. But the morning of his eighteenth birthday, just after midnight, he walked to the nearest train tracks and hopped on an empty rail car. He'd wound up in Jackson, Wyoming and applied for the first job he saw a *help wanted* sign for—detailing cars and trucks at a huge truck stop car wash.

His boss, Bill Miller, recognized his strong work ethics immediately as well as his lack of money for food or housing. After three days of sleeping on the truck stop bathroom floor, he was awakened one night by a gentle tap on his shoulder, fed and then shown to a tiny room upstairs above the cafe that contained a single half bed—nothing more.

Drake kept that job and bed for the next three years—saving every dime he made except what he spent for food and for the purchase of a pickup that boss Miller—as he was called—helped him choose.

Boss Miller's wife, Sue, made sure the holidays over the years were made special—as much as Drake would allow. For the most part, he kept to himself, choosing to be alone.

But the sadness that she witnessed on him so consistently caused her to take every opportunity she found to try and drag conversation from him about his background. Finally—the first spark of excitement shown in his youthful green eyes when he'd revealed his love for horses and ranching—the fact that he'd been raised to rope and break colts from the time he was ten years old.

The Millers decided to try and give their young, favorite employee a chance to step up in life—to work at a job he knew and obviously loved.

After speaking to Andy Parker at the Cowboy Church where they had attended for several years, Drake Henson began work at High Point Dude Ranch and as an extra hand for the Double OO.

The Millers lost their best car detailer, but privately high-fived each other in their joy of seeing Drake smile for the first time in three years. Sue cried when he drove out of their truck stop parking lot.

Ben Rivers carried the last saddle into the tack room and set it on its rack, then gathered up the bridles and hung them on wooden pegs above the saddles. "Maybe we should look around for Mr. Walton, Drake. Make sure he's okay. It hasn't been long since he was in the hospital."

"I was thinking that, too, Ben. But the way these people around here feel about each other—I figure there's at least two ten-man posses out searching now."

Ben laughed. "Probably so. I'm on chuck wagon detail for supper. Guess I'll go check with the kitchen and see what I need to do."

"Okay. Later, man."

Ben left the barn and discretely glanced around the grounds as he headed toward the Brandon's ranch house. Jenny Luke, Judd and Toni's young daughter had been helping out around here the past few days. He had known her for as long as he'd been coming here to church but had only recently *noticed* her in a different way. He'd just noticed how pretty she was. Seemed she had grown up a lot lately—at least her body was something to look at.

At age eighteen, Ben had graduated high school five months ago in May and hired on for High Point's busy summer season. He didn't have a background in any aspect of ranching but was a willing and fast learner. Andy Parker had vouched for him to his Uncle Donny and then took him under his wing of responsibility.

Ben Rivers parents owned a small mom and pop cafe on the edge of Jackson Hole where he'd worked since he was old enough to say *welcome to Rivers.* Before he was out of elementary school, Ben had proven to have a unique gift in art. By the time he was in high school, he'd sold several of his drawings that were displayed on the cafe walls. But it was the sketch he'd done of an aged cowboy, his gray-haired cowgirl and their little senior sidekick pup, Bonny, wearing her tiny, well used straw hat that he'd purposefully done for Mr. and Mrs. Walton right after Hank was released from the hospital—that

Ben was most proud of. He'd known the elder couple since he was small and had called them Gramps and Granny right along with the Brandon kids back then.

The sight of the framed gift caused tears to instantly trickle onto their wrinkled cheeks, bringing a first-time recognition of the possibilities of his special gift.

But right now—drawing was the last thing on his teen aged hormone-pumping brain. Hay riding with a bunch of squealing kids to make sure they didn't fall off the wagon or walking behind a posse of the same brainless pony trail-riders was pure torture when he wanted to daydream about Jenny. Even the thought of her name made shivers roll through his middle.

When he spied her carrying a large pot of beans from the back door of the house to the chuck wagon, he eagerly rushed to intercept her.

"Let me carry that for you, Jenny. It looks heavy."

"Thank you. But I'm stronger than I look."

He winked at her as he grasped the side handles of the pot—his hands covering hers long enough to bring a deep blush to her cheeks. Her gaze went to the ground and she turned quickly and headed back toward the kitchen.

When she glanced back at him, he was standing there watching her walk away, the flirty twinkle in his eyes making her cheeks burn.

A second later, she plowed face first into Andy Parker's chest when he came out of the back door of his parent's house.

"Whoa there, little bit. I didn't mean to run you over."

"I'm okay," she muttered as she hurried around him and disappeared inside the kitchen.

He glanced at her hasty retreat, then back at the figure striding off with a pot of beans. The scene he thought he just saw—he really hoped he didn't see.

"Mr. Walton?"

Hank twisted his body around just enough to get a glimpse of the figure standing a few feet behind him, then turned his focus back onto the still water in the creek.

"Hello, Drake. Come have a seat."

Drake walked over to his side and squatted down beside him. "Just letting you know supper is about ready."

Hank cut his eyes at the young new ranch hand and grinned. "I figured my wife was having a little fit about now."

He grinned broadly. "Well…that, too."

That brought a nod and a chuckle. "Sure is peaceful out here this time of evenin. Just thought I'd catch up on some thinkin."

"I guess you're feeling all right?"

"Better than ever. Swelling in this shoulder and arm is about all gone. I imagine you boys will be glad for me to get back to doing the cooking."

"Well, sir, I wasn't here before you got banned from that, but I figure I'll make somebody a good wife someday with all the culinary skills I've acquired lately."

Hank howled with laughter. "You just don't ever tell her about this and I won't either."

"Deal."

"I'll be along shortly."

"I'll tell Mrs. Walton you're all right." Drake headed back up the creek bank wondering how some men manage to turn out like this old gentleman—as well as most all the men from this ranch—versus his dad.

Hank picked up a quarter-sized rock off the ground beside him and chunked it into the middle of the cordoned-off swimming hole. As he watched the ripples in the water, they seemed to form the faces of his loving mom and dad smiling at him as though time rolled backward for a few moments.

Henry and Jill Rhea were two of the most gentle and peaceful human beings Buck Rhea had ever known. He was their only child. Never once in his life did either of them ever raise a hand or their voice to him. Love and respect was shown to him every day of his life as far back as he could recall. They were in their late forties when he was born and taught him by example how to treat other people with dignity no matter who they were. He wondered if the loving and charitable character they were known for—in the end—brought violence and death into their home. Maybe to some degree, but Buck Rhea, their rookie cop son, was the catalyst that started the rampage against them. It was his mistake—his unthinking action of pulling his glock and firing—killing the son of one of the most notorious drug lords in the state of California.

Hank recalled taking a bullet during the ruckus but had no memory of pulling his own gun—let alone killing a man. These memories had been squelched deep inside his soul all these years but didn't want to let him alone these days.

After the Rhea's were murdered in their small farmhouse—Buck entered the witness protection program and moved to Jackson Hole, Wyoming—as Hank Walton.

Close to forty years had passed since then and Jesse Brandon offered to take him to view the grave sites of his family. He hadn't been able to attend their funerals or see the graves.

"Whew." Hank's chin jerked hard and he swiped at the unwelcome tears streaming down his leathery-aged cheeks. "Whew." His heart was broken.

He wasn't too crazy about the idea of going back there at first, but it seemed something was pulling on his heartstrings today. He couldn't shake the pictures of those gentle, smiling faces that had formed in the circling creek water. He hadn't been able to see them— to remember how they looked—in all these long years. Today he couldn't move them from his vision. Almost as though they were trying to visit with him.

Today was the Brandon's *end of dude season* thank-you celebration to all the families and hands who had worked from one ranch to the other, as needed. This year had been exceptional with everyone pitching in for the last half of the season after Hank's blood clot episode.

He was back to cooking and had been in the Brandon's kitchen since before daylight preparing cakes and cookies and his famous cauldron of chicken and dumplings.

Granny Martha set out ingredients for whatever he was mixing up and kept the pots, bowls and utensils washed and the countertops wiped down as he mixed and poured and de-boned several large pressure-cooked chickens. His homemade chicken broth was the secret to his popular chicken and dumplin recipe and he took great pride in keeping it under wraps—except for Martha, of course. In fact, today he let her season the broth without his help.

"Mmm! That's better than mine, young lady."

Martha pressed her hand into her chest. "Oh my—are you dying or is it me and this is your way of tellin me?"

Hank laughed out loud. "Hate to break it to you, sweetheart of mine, but we both are—sooner or later. But if you won't get in any big hurry about it, I won't either."

"You two are having entirely too much fun in here. Now knock it off. I'm gettin jealous." Jesse walked into the kitchen from the hallway and out the back door without slowing down.

Hank stepped over and planted a hard kiss on her mouth. "I'll show him *knock it off.*"

Martha giggled and headed to the sink to wash another few dishes. She had to admit, the change in Hank Walton since he came so close to death a few weeks ago was to her liking, although he was never, ever harsh or complaining. But he had taken on a childlike playfulness—fun-loving to the point of mischievous. Her kind of man—with extras. What would she do without him? And yet, she was aware, more now than ever, that one of them would leave the other behind someday. She refused to think about it any further.

That afternoon, Judd and Toni saddled up and rode out to look over their pastures of Hereford cattle and enjoy a few hours of riding-time together doing what they both loved best.

Toni was an expert colt breaker—spoken of by some as a genuine horse whisperer. Raised from ten years old by her bachelor uncle,

John Baxter, in Texas—he'd revealed his well-kept secret of horse whispering to her after he recognized her inner sense for the *sacred calling*. And she believed, as well, that's what it is—sacred and not to be taken lightly. She had never shared the secret that was entrusted to her so long ago, but she *had* been called on a few times through the years to exercise that gift. She would always demand privacy for her and the unruly horse, like Uncle John had taught her—and not once did it ever fail to work. She did wonder if the secret would end when her life did. There wasn't anyone she felt drawn to share it with—no one who would give it the honor it deserved.

"That far-off look in your eyes tells me you are not taking in the beauty of our surroundings out here." Judd had sidestepped his gelding right up against his wife's mount and smiled questioningly into her face while their horses continued walking.

When she raised her head and leaned toward him, he bent and kissed her lips softly.

"I was thinking about Uncle John—missing him a little bit today."

He covered her hand with his leather gloved palm and squeezed. "He was a good man. He would have loved this place."

She giggled. "I wonder what he would have thought about the two of us finding each other again—becoming grandparents, no less."

Judd grinned broadly. "Oh, he knows."

"You really think so."

"Yes, I believe God has some means *up there,*" he pointed a finger Heavenward, "of letting the positive parts of our lives, at least, be shared with those who care to know. Do you know what he probably said when he learned about us?"

She thought for a second before looking up at him, then both of them said in unison, *"Well I'll be jiggered."*

It took a full minute for their laughter to die down.

"Yep, that old man was a card. He threatened to whip my butt nine ways from Sunday when he found out I was hanging out too close to his little girl—brat that you were."

Fourteen-year-old—brat, mister."

"Don't remind me. I would have deserved every knot he raised on me—and he would have if I hadn't hightailed it out of there."

For the next hour, they rode down fence lines and across pastures, weaving through the heifers and last spring's babies. A few late calves should be born about now, but they hadn't spotted any yet.

Toni noticed a couple of mamas off in the distance, a good half mile or more away near the base of a heavy pine timberline that ran horizontal along the base of the Wind River Mountains. They both seemed agitated about something. They were far away, but Toni's mothering instincts told her they were having a problem.

She reined to a stop and pointed toward them. After a few seconds studying the horizon, Judd nodded and without a word, they headed that way at a safe gallop.

The mamas were crying—their udder's full. When they stopped their horses, one of the frantic heifer's charged at them, but turned away at Judd's loud voice and lariat swinging towards her. The other one stood still and challenged the horse riders by shaking her head up and down in warning.

Toni moved around the pair in a wide circle, slowly urging her mount closer in from behind as she searched the tall grasses and bushes. She wasn't surprised when she spotted the problem, but still had to fight the tightening in her chest for the poor mamas who were bawling for their babies. Remains of two newborn calves were not much more than a couple of bloody pieces and parts in separate spots several yards apart.

"Judd."

Giving a wide berth to the angry white-faced pair, he made his way to the back side of the brush where he instantly saw the carnage. He could see Toni was upset, so he squared his shoulders and kept his emotions tucked away.

"They wandered out too far—too close to the timber. Probably the work of wolves."

She shuddered. "Maybe we should run a fence closer in so they can't come this far again."

"I'll look into that. We've never had them stray over in this area." He adjusted his straw Stetson on his head and sighed deeply after twisting his left wrist to glance at his watch.

"Should we try to drive them back toward the herd?"

He shook his head. "If they're forced to leave from here, they'll just come back looking for those babies. They'll figure it out in a day or two and go back on their own. Let's head on back. We need to join the party at High Point."

Toni reined her horse around and led the way at a fast walk, then broke into a lope. The bawling mama cows were getting to her. Right now, a party was the last place she wanted to go. She'd seen enough of these situations to toughen up her emotions—almost a lifetime worth—but, today she couldn't hold it together. Tears were spilling over and blowing back into the sides of her hair. She was pretty sure she knew why.

Judd and Toni were the last to arrive for the shindig but were just in time for the lineup to the large table of food that set on the far end of the pavilion floor. Picnic tables were moved onto the grass—several flood lights were positioned around the grounds to help provide a party atmosphere after the sun set within the next couple of hours.

Jesse stepped purposefully into the middle of the pavilion carrying the dinner bell from Grandpa Hank's chuck wagon. The loud clanging brought everyone to silent attention, except a few squealing kids chasing each other around the yard.

"Folks," he began in a loud, strong voice, but was interrupted by a member of the band striding over to hand him a wireless microphone. "Hello," he boomed into it. "Whoa…sorry about that. I'm not used to these new-fangled contraptions."

Laughter rose up through the crowd that had gathered close in.

"Brother, you really need to get out more," Donny Brandon quipped

More laughter.

"Pipe down, squirt. I'm still bigger than you." He paused a second while the chuckles died away. "I just want to welcome everybody to our annual *thank you* party. My family appreciates every one of you who worked so hard for us this year...some of you went way beyond the call when we got a little desperate around here. It's great to see Clint and Abby and little David back for a visit in our part of the world. So, lets thank the Lord Jesus for this day and all that food there and for another successful year."

All hats came off, kids were quieted and Jesse prayed. Within fifteen minutes, everyone was seated and lots of eating, laughter and visiting went on for the next couple of hours.

As darkness fell, the lights lit up a large area of the ranch yard. Just before the band began to play, Les Kane stood at his place at the picnic table and gently clanged on the dinner bell he'd borrowed from Jesse. When he had the group's attention, he stepped behind Kaitlyn, who was seated on the bench, and placed his hands on her shoulders.

"If you all will indulge an old man for another minute, I have an announcement. Since everyone here is all pretty much family, my wife agreed to let me say this." He glanced down at the top of her head and swallowed hard, then scanned the wondering faces. "We wanted to share our good news...that our prayers have been answered. Come next April, we're having a baby."

Amid gasps and squeals and applause, Kaitlyn was covered up with hugs—Backslaps and handshakes rushed around Les.

Even amid the smiles and happy tears surrounding the moment, Judd Luke was keenly aware of Toni's half-heartedness over the news. The crease between her eyes matched a look that was set deep in her gaze that he couldn't quite define. This wasn't like his spunky, lighthearted little bride of two decades. Normally, she would have been squealing and dancing a jig over this news.

It was ten minutes before the excitement settled down around the middle-aged parents-to-be, only to start up again with an excited slip of the tongue when Abby Berry whispered to Kaitlyn that she was expecting again—in April.

"What! Oh, Abby...you and Clint, too...in April!"—came excitedly out of Kaitlyn's mouth before she thought better of it.

Toni didn't move nor react toward her daughter. When the others turned their surprised laughter toward Abby and Clint, she only stared almost with a look of horror added to her already strange deep-set visage.

Abby was laughing with joy as she rushed to her mom and apologized for the slip. "I meant to tell you and Daddy first. I'm sorry. It just came out in all the excitement."

Toni gave her a wide smile and tight hug. "You look so happy, Ab. That's what matters to me."

After a few more rounds of hugs and congratulatory back slaps, the pavilion filled up with dancers two-stepping to the country music that filled the air.

Judd was tapping his boots, itching to dance as he scanned the area for his dance partner.

AJ walked up and reached to shake his hand. "Congratulations. Hear you're going to be grandpa again."

"Thank you, AJ. That's the only bad thing about kids marrying and moving away. Those grand babies go, too."

Daisy Corry snagged AJ for a dance, cutting the conversation off short. Judd still hadn't spotted Toni, but Andy noticed him intently scanning faces and danced toward him as he held Rachel on his hip, twirling her around to the music.

"Looking for Toni?" He hollered as he rounded the corner in front of Judd.

He nodded.

"Saw her walking toward the barn a minute ago."

"Thanks." He headed that way, remembering the strange look in her eyes. It wasn't like her to be this upset over the cow/calf situation they ran onto earlier. Toni had been around that all her life. She'd always taken the good with the bad and dealt with it. *Was she sick?*

That thought made him lengthen his stride. It was dark near the barn, except for a dim night-light beside the tack room door. When he stepped fully inside, he stood still to listen. The horses were quiet. When he started to turn and go back outside, he heard a faint sound like crying coming from the back row of stalls.

A minute later, he found Toni on her knees in the back corner of the walkway. He went to her and squatted down beside her, his hand resting on her back.

"Honey?" This was not like her at all. He gently grasped her upper arms and pulled her to him. "Baby, you're scaring me. I need you to talk to me." He held her close while she attempted to pull herself together.

"I'm sorry, Cowboy. I'm so sorry."

He had no idea what she thought she had to apologize for, but he dearly loved the sound of *Cowboy* every time she called him that. When they'd first known each other as kids on her Uncle John's ranch in Texas, she only knew him as Cowboy and he had tagged her as Pigtails. That was a long time ago. And now that he thought about it—she only called him Cowboy now when she was either in a very playful mood or when she was feeling desperate or scared.

He pressed her tighter into his chest. "What for," he whispered. "Please don't tell me *you* are the one who robbed that bank down in Texas last month."

She socked his shoulder and he knew she was trying not to let him know she wanted to laugh.

"Ow! I'll take that as a no."

She pulled back from his hold and swiped her hands across her cheeks. "Everybody's...preg...nant and...I dreamed the baby was born dead and I had thought such horrible thoughts...that..."

"Whoa, lets slow down. I'm not following this. Now...when did you have a bad dream?"

"Two nights ago. When I saw the pieces of the dead baby calves today, the dream came at me...like it was real...because I had those horrible thoughts. I thought about," she covered her face with her hands and moaned, "about abortion. How could I think such a thing?"

Judd was scrambling in his head to put her words into some sort of order. She must have already known Abby was pregnant again. The dream and then seeing the remains of the newborn calves— "Honey, you had a really bad dream and then saw the calves. Everybody is fine. Abby is healthy and we're getting a new grand baby."

"We're getting a...baby."

"Yes, we are. This is something to celebrate. Sounds like that old devil has been playing games with you. You had a nightmare and then thoughts of abortion...and dead calves."

Toni was quiet now and seemed to be back to herself—looking into his face with her normal strength and clarity.

"Cowboy...we're having a baby."

"Yes, Grandma, we sure are."

She watched his face, feeling her eyes burning again.

"Judd...*I'm* pregnant."

A flash of shock, then more shock coated his face. "Oh...my...God in Heaven!" He shook his head. Now it all made sense. A mixture of thoughts were jumbling through his brain at once—diapers, bottles, baby food, 2 A.M.— It had been nearly fifteen years since they did this. They were grandparents now.

"Then it hit him. He returned his gaze on her. "Toni, did you have thoughts of...of aborting our child?"

The question felt like a knife slicing her heart. But his expression was gentle and kind. "The thought was in my head. When I realized I was pregnant...I didn't want to be. I didn't want to start over." She lowered her face, unable to look at the most precious gift God had ever given her—not after what she had just revealed to him.

He grasped the sides of her face with both hands and raised her gaze back to his. "You had thoughts of abortion and then had a nightmare that the baby was born dead?"

She nodded and squeezed her eyes shut as tears rolled.

"Toni, right now, do you want this baby?"

"With all my heart and soul. I can't believe I could have ever thought something so horrible."

"My thoughts just now when you told me you were pregnant was...no, thanks! I don't really relish doing the diaper stuff again. That was my first thought. Lord, Grandma...we're old! We both know full well that thoughts like that are evil darts thrown into our heads by satan himself. Your thought wasn't so different from mine...you just didn't plan on starting over. That dream was

33

evil…probably triggered by your guilt at having that thought. You know, Pigtails, we aren't starting over at all. We simply aren't finished with the family God needs us to have."

Her widened eyes were glued to his, hardly believing the loving understanding of this big cowboy.

0   "Look, woman, I'm trying to *Pastor Judd*—or *Dr. Phil* you here. How am I doing so far?"

A grin spread across her lips and Judd's eyes twinkled with suppressed laughter.

"By the way, when's this little bundle of diapers—I mean—*joy* — due."

Toni burst out laughing then and choked out, "Ap…ril."

He squinted his eyes and stared off in the darkness of the barn for a few seconds before it hit. Laughter exploded out of both of them until they laid over on each other, holding their stomachs.

***

CHAPTER THREE

By the time they returned to the pavilion, they'd been missed by most of the party. Strolling up with arms around each other, faces flushed and still grinning like two school kids—the teasing was endless.

"Where have you two been?" Abby asked. Her voice was high pitched and close to accusing.

Jesse and Laura, Les and Kaitlyn, Donny and Reeny, Andy and Summer and others who had been getting concerned about their absence, gathered around them.

"Somebody tell that bartender—*no more for these two.*" Donny chuckled.

Judd laughed. "Do we look that bad?"

"Worse," Jesse confirmed. "Did we miss out on something fun?"

"Dad! Mom!" Abby exclaimed.

Judd knew they were going to have to give up an explanation. They had been out of pocket for an hour and then showed up looking like two cats with feathers sticking out their teeth. "Alright…alright." He put up a hand, knowing this was probably as good a time as any. He looked at Toni for a little help, but she just signaled for him to go ahead. "Somebody get Jenny for us. She needs to be here for this."

Andy moved toward the band and told them to hold the next song for a few minutes. While they finished the last chorus, Andy turned and spotted Jenny Luke wrapped up in Ben Rivers arms until she could hardly be seen. He stepped into the dance area between them and her parents view, vowing to clue young Ben in on a *fourteen-year-old* fact—first chance he got.

"Young lady, your mom and dad need you over there," he pointed their direction.

Ben dropped his arms from around her when he caught the glare Andy shot his way and went off to sit down with Drake and AJ.

Andy followed Jenny to the small group gathered around the Lukes.

"Well, folks, I don't know if this is the proper time or not, but I'd rather let everyone in on the news I just received than risk my preaching license to..." he glanced at Toni— "a racy rumor from my favorite congregation."

Laughter sang through the group.

"It's actually a long story—but you're only getting the short, most important version. Abby...Jen, apparently God wasn't finished with our immediate family. This took us by surprise, to say the least, but in the midst of a few tears and a lot of hysterical laughter—which is why we look like we do, your mama just told me she's expecting a baby."

He waited for the initial shock of gasps and hugs and tears to subside—happy to see that both of their girls were genuinely excited—and then, he tossed out the fact— "oh, and on a side note, the baby's due in April."

A few days later, Jesse decided it was time to make arrangements for a trip to California. Hank had agreed to go, but insisted Martha go with him. Reluctantly, she agreed, even though she was afraid of air transportation—but with the stipulation that Laura go with them.

"So, what do you think, Mrs. Brandon? Want to double date across the country with the Waltons? No pressure or anything, but this whole mission hinges on your answer." With Hank's permission, Jesse had shown Laura the newspaper clipping and told her about Hank's past.

She didn't have to think about it more than a few seconds. "Of course I'll go. I would be honored to do this for Hank." Her eyes glistened and she laughed a little as she reached for a napkin on the kitchen island. "Sorry. My emotions are all jumbled up. I'm happy for him and sad at the same time."

He gazed at his wife—the compassion she had inside her for the trouble in other people's lives was pure and strong. She was always on the lookout for what she could do to help somebody. It didn't surprise him that she was teary-eyed over Hank. He knew this moment was just the preliminary to the flood that was coming.

"I know how you feel. I'm sure there'll be a few tears shed before this is over. And that's all right. They're way overdue."

Laura knew he was talking about Hank. She came around the counter and walked into her husband's arms where he sat on a stool, knees spread. He rubbed her back and shoulders, then held her face between his large palms and unhurriedly kissed her full lips.

"How can one little female, so delicate and gorgeous, be so strong on the inside."

She held his gaze with her own, letting him see the strength of her love for him through it. "You know, Jess, there's not much down time with you. You either make me laugh or you put a lump in my throat. But always—always…you make me feel loved."

He pulled her into him and held her in a tight hug for a long time.

"That wasn't so bad, Martha…was it?" Laura chided Granny Martha as they exited the ramp and entered the east coast airport. "It was almost boring…not even an air pocket to make us catch our breath." She was giddy with excitement of just having completed the first leg of her and Jesse's mini vacation.

"It was all right, I guess, but we have to get back on that dern thing to go home." She was frowning and Laura sensed real fear that glanced at her.

She wrapped her arm around her best friend and partner in crime, as she whispered to her, "God rode with us, sweet lady. And… He's going back with us when we go home. I booked His flight myself. We are so safe."

Martha nodded her head just as Hank reached for her hand. She had been so panicked at the thought of flying—she hadn't given proper notice of this distinguished looking cowboy gentleman until this moment. He was wearing a white, long sleeved western shirt, new denim Levis and his Sunday boots and Silver Belly Stetson. He was clean shaven, with a neatly trimmed mustache.

Hank Walton was a big man and the way he carried himself through the airport, back straight, shoulders squared—walking like a man on a mission—he looked like he'd left a few years back at the ranch.

For the first time since preparing for this trip, Martha was feeling good about the new clothes Laura had talked her into on a quick trip to town the day before. Her new layered haircut and touch of makeup was long overdue according to her friend who was like a sister. Feeling the squeeze her husband just gave her hand and that look when he glanced down at her just now—she felt a youthful exuberance stand her up a little straighter.

Martha had never been one to pay significant attention to her looks. She periodically trimmed the length off the bottom of her own white/gray hair, but makeup was never important.

When Hank noticed a section of the wall they were walking past was mirrored—he stopped suddenly and turned to face it, guiding Martha to face it beside him. He placed an arm around her shoulders and leaned into her. "I had no idea we could gussie-up this good. Just look at us."

For once, she didn't make a wise crack and try to be funny. She loved the way he never failed to laugh at her witty remarks, but she couldn't go there this time. They were gazing almost trance-like at each other in the glass wall. His heart was drumming like a schoolboy and the way she was looking at him—he knew she was feeling it, too. They smiled slightly at each other before turning and continuing down the hall.

Jesse and Laura were strolling slowly up ahead of them, trying hard to pretend they hadn't witnessed what they just witnessed—but that sweet image would be etched into both their minds forever.

It was dark when Jesse parked their rental car in front of the Hamlet Estates Inn. They were all exhausted and retired to their rooms, knowing tomorrow would be a stressful day.

"I can't remember the last time I stayed in a motel." Hank set the suitcase and large overnight bag on the floor. "But I believe they've gotten a little fancier." His gaze traveled slowly around the room. Two taupe leather recliners set side by side with a glass topped lamp table between them. A TV faced them against the opposite wall—a huge TV that looked more like it belonged in a movie theater. The other half of the room was filled with a king-sized bed that was calling his name. He stepped inside the doorway of the bathroom to see a glass shower and separate bathtub similar to the fancy ones in Donny's and Andy's and Beau's houses. He thought he might enjoy all this more under different circumstances, but Martha would feel like a queen in here, he knew.

He heard the lock on the door bolt shut behind him and half turned in time to see Martha reaching her arms out to him. One hand yanked his hat off and tossed it onto a side chair, his other hand grasped her around the waist and pulled her in. They stood in that spot in a tight embrace for a full five minutes. They had grown closer—more quietly serious with each other since Hank's brush with death. Neither had truly thought much about how it would feel if one lost the other—if one was left alone suddenly to face every day and night alone again. Words didn't seem that important to convey their feelings to each other. It was all in moments like this—touching, long tight hugs and the deliberate, purposeful depth of looking into the other's eyes. *Really* looking. They saw each other in a way that almost transcended the mortal lives they were living right now. Both were aware that something felt different between them—something good—something beyond themselves.

When they pulled back from each other, Hank could see the tired in his wife's face. "Let's get ready for bed. I'll make coffee in that little pot over there and we'll talk awhile."

She nodded and got what she needed out of the suitcase before closing herself up in the bathroom. When she came out a few minutes later, the bed covers were turned down and pillows were propped up against the headboard.

"Just in time, my girl." He was dressed in white T-shirt and sweatpants, standing beside the bed holding two smoking cups.

When she was settled against the pillows, he handed her a cup and then went around to his side and slid in beside her. They were silent for a while, savoring the hot coffee and cool sheets.

When he finally set his cup on the bedside table, he turned slightly toward her, resting an arm along the top of her pillows. Her shag-cut hair was messy and bouncy, touching her shoulders in places. He ran his fingers through it, amazed at the softness.

"Did I tell you how much I like your hair?"

She cut her eyes at him and shook her head.

"Well, I *do* like it and you look different and beautiful in your make-up." He noticed she hadn't washed it off.

"I'm glad you like it, but don't get used to it. I don't have time to do up my face every day."

He chuckled, "I wouldn't want you to. But when we were standing in front of that big mirror at the airport, I realized something about us."

"What's that?"

"We're not so old."

She looked at him with widened eyes and he thought she was going to burst out laughing.

"Seriously, woman, look at you. Your new haircut and a little makeup took years off you. I think *you* were making me look better in that mirror, but you run around the ranch all day like a little hyper chicken and I don't have any trouble working from a saddle all day either when I'm needed."

Neither said a word for a long minute.

She set her coffee on her bedside table then and twisted around to wrap both her arms around him and looked him in the eyes. "Hank, you have no idea how happy you just made me. I saw us in the mirror, too. What I saw surprised me. We looked like some couple…besides us. And…I don't *feel* old."

She laid her head on his chest and felt her eyes burn as he caressed her cheek and threaded his rough, calloused fingers through her unusually silky gray hair to pull it away from her eyes.

"You know," he paused a moment, "neither of us got much chance to enjoy being in love as young people do." He lay his head back on the pillows and continued fingering her hair. "By the time we got together, we had been handed the roles of Gramps and Granny to a growing family of babies." His voice broke and he paused a few moments. "That's the greatest blessing I've ever had and I thank God every day for it."

He glanced down at the top of her head and smiled slightly. "You come right after that, Ms. Walton, just so you know."

She nodded approval and patted his mostly flat belly. "I can live with that blessing, Mr. Walton."

"I guess," he continued, "I'm feeling like me and you should take a little more time for…us…when there's down time at the ranch. Take a week here and there and kick up our heels. We've only got *us* for just so long. We can't know when life will suddenly change…for either of us. Everything you've ever known or loved can be gone in the blink…"

"Hank…" she looked up and placed a hand on his cheek to stop his rush of words. She understood. "Hank…I'm here and I'll be beside you every step of the way tomorrow. You'll be all right. I'll help you be all right. I've been helping you since the day I shook your chili spoon all over you and asked for a date to the hot tub, and then, proposed marriage to you and gave you my secret chicken broth recipe and…"

"Whoa…whoa…hold it right there. *I* gave *you…my* secret chicken broth recipe."

"Yeah, well, that makes it mine now. Same difference."

At that, he leaned his head back and howled with laughter. "Maybe. And maybe I need to take some of that sass out of you, little gal."

Quick as lightening, she rolled away from him and reached for the only lamp that was on—and flipped it off. "Thought I was going to have to ask for that, too, cowboy!"

She slid back under the covers and rolled into his arms to the music of his laughter.

Laura and Martha went into the County Clerk's office downtown the next morning, leaving their men drinking coffee across the street in the Drinks and Eats. Even though it had been over four decades, they chose to take every precaution getting in and out of the area without drawing any notice.

The middle-aged lady behind the desk looked up the information for Henry and Jill Rhea's burial place and handed Laura the information she'd scribbled on a notepad. The woman seemed slightly curious about her and Martha when she handed over the paper. Her eyes seemed to study each of their faces for a split second each before nonchalantly offering— "Those are very old graves, but that cemetery has always been well maintained. Is this family you're searching for?"

Laura smiled. "Oh, no. I'm just doing a little ancestry work on certain names. Thank you for your help."

"Yes, mam. You're welcome."

As soon as they were outside the office door, Martha asked, "Did she seem a little odd acting toward us?"

"No, I don't think so. We're just a little on edge because of Hank's circumstances. But we'll be headed home in just a few hours. Let's round up our guys and go do this." Laura gave Martha's back a comforting pat as they exited the courthouse.

Hank remembered where that particular cemetery was and directed Jesse to it. He had patrolled this area during his time on the city police force. It wasn't more than a couple miles from the side street and warehouse where his nightmare began—where he'd killed the son of a Mafia gangster. He didn't feel anxious at all about being here—but, to the contrary, peaceful.

The only difference he noticed on this long road running alongside the cemetery was how much bigger it was—forty years of more burial plots. There was a new subdivision of large homes built across the street that used to be pastureland. He smiled as he recalled the countless number of teens parking late at night—spread out all over the grassy grounds. He'd used the spot himself as a teen. Other than that, it all looked the same.

Jesse pulled through the open iron gates and drove slowly up and down the roads that wound through the endless rows of headstones. Laura had directions to the area of the graves they were looking for, but for safety sake, he veered away from that part for a short while. He'd only seen two vehicles in the whole place, one belonging to a young woman who was sitting beside a fresh mound of dirt covered in flowers and the other was a service truck for the cemetery with two young men covering potholes with gravel.

He finally pulled over when he found the row number and they got out to walk the few yards to where the Rhea's stone should be.

Holding hands, Hank and Martha headed that way as Jesse continuously scanned the area for visitors, Laura standing beside him.

Only one other person could be seen in the area as far as the eye could see—an elderly woman sat on a visitor's bench about two headstone rows across from where Hank and Martha now stood. Apparently, they found the graves.

After a long minute, Hank embraced his wife and she quickly headed back toward Jesse and Laura.

"He wants to be alone for a while." She fought to control her trembling chin as she brushed tears off her cheeks. "It's a very nice double stone with some beautiful and fairly fresh flowers in the center of it."

Jesse nodded and walked off looking at the old stones with old family names. Laura knew his emotions were getting raw, but the same question hit all their minds—who had put up such a costly stone? And flowers? The other graves were virtually bare of anything resembling a flower—live or fake.

Hank had dropped to his knees beside the headstone and Laura steered Martha back toward the car.

Jesse watched from a distance where he walked farther into the hallowed grounds. Then, in a moment, he froze in his tracks as he noticed the elderly lady walking slowly with a cane and carrying a bouquet of colorful, fresh flowers. She seemed to be making her way toward Hank, probably to offer him comfort. But Jesse headed in that direction as did Laura and Martha until they were all within hearing distance of Hank.

The woman stopped beside the Rhea's headstone on the opposite side from where Hank knelt and without a word, exchanged the partially wilted flowers with the vibrant new ones.

Hank looked up to view the smiling face of a woman, probably well into her eighties. A gray bun wound tightly at the back of her neck, matched her solid gray ankle length dress. She held the wilted flowers out to keep the water from dripping on her as she leaned on her cane.

The others had now moved in behind Hank and he stood up—his leathery face wet with tears.

The woman glanced at each of them, then back to Hank. "Mr. Buck Rhea?"

Hank remained silent, not knowing what he should do. Jesse took a step closer to him, partially shielding him from her and fully prepared to launch himself into the woman if she made a wrong move. His eyes darted around the area. *How in sam hill could this happen in one moment of a day after forty years?*

"Forgive me for this intrusion. I've made you all fear me, but please let me explain. My name is Karlotta Montella. I'm your friend...not an enemy. I have prayed for many years for this moment...to meet you...so I could properly apologize for what my family did to you and to your precious family."

When she saw Hank's eyes widen, she hurriedly continued. "I hated what my family had done. I grieved for you and for them. "She nodded at the grave. "I didn't know what happened to the police officer who killed my brother, but I knew they never found you because I listened to their conversations." She looked intently into Hank's eyes. "Mr. Rhea...they are all dead now. I am the only one left of my family. I bought the marker and I put flowers here. I didn't know what else to do." She turned slightly and waved the flowers in the direction of the gate. "I live just across the way there. It was a terrible thing they did." She lowered her face and was silent.

Hank managed to loosen himself from the shock—realizing the enormity of what she just said. He stepped closer to her, walking around the back side of the stone, but had to work to find his voice. He cleared his throat, taking a minute to process this woman.

"Mam...Karlotta...are you telling me you bought this gravestone and ...kept flowers on it?"

She nodded without looking up. "Thirty-five years." She met his eyes again.

Hank shot Jesse an incredulous look and glanced at Martha's and Laura's shocked widened eyes. They all remained silent.

"But how...how did you know I was coming here today?"

She glanced toward the others, then looked away for a moment before looking back at Hank. "I'm not sure you could understand how this happened."

"Well, I'd like you to give me the *chance* to understand."

She lowered her gaze to the ground, then slowly looked away and stared out into the expanse of the cemetery—It was clear she was visualizing something other than the present sights around her. She swallowed hard, thought hard and fought hard with her inner self. Finally, she stopped fighting and glanced around the grounds. "I need to sit down."

Laura spotted a bench a few yards away. As soon as she pointed at it, Jesse and Hank got it and set it immediately behind her, both of them steadying her until she sat down. She leaned forward partially resting her weight on her cane.

After the two men carried a second bench from nearby, Laura and Martha shared it—all of them turning full attention to Karlotta Montella.

***

CHAPTER FOUR

It was apparent that neither Judd nor Toni Luke had noticed the exchanges between Ben Rivers and their young daughter, Jenny.

Andy didn't know how Judd might react and he didn't want to make a mountain of a molehill—as the saying goes—but maybe he could discreetly let Ben know the score and thwart a probable bad situation before it went any further.

A supper of barbecue sandwiches had been served to the hands from the chuck wagon—manned by Andy's wife, Summer and Donny and Reeny. After cleanup, the ranch had settled into an unusual quiet. With the absence of the patriarch and matriarch Brandon's and Gramps and Granny Martha—the place felt empty. It would be difficult to keep this ranch thriving without them. The spark was gone.

Andy stepped up in his dually and headed out to the bunkhouse where Ben stayed occasionally rather than driving back into town where he lived with his parents. He had seen him go that direction carrying his sandwich with him.

Ben heard the soft nicker of a newcomer calling a greeting to the gelding Drake had stalled in the holding pen on the side of the bunkhouse. He glanced at himself in the mirror beside the door, deciding to leave his hat off as he went out to meet Jenny and halter her horse for her.

"Glad you made it over." Ben let his eyes take in her slender form—her pretty, timid face and then winked at her as he unhooked a halter and rope from the fence post and took the reins from her. He deliberately slid his fingers over hers in the process. When he saw her cheeks pink, he knew she was feeling an attraction to him—his heart rate kicked up a notch.

After he tied her gelding and loosened the saddle girth, he took Jenny's hand and led her to the porch swing that hung from the awning rafters by two heavy duty chains. Mitch Corry had hung it up for his new bride, Daisy, while they waited for the larger and more modernized bunkhouse to be built a few acres behind this one.

"You want a coke. There's Sprite in there, too."

She shook her head. "No thanks. I can't stay long. My parents don't know I rode all the way over here. So, do you live here?"

He sat down beside her. "Not really. I live in town, but I stay out here now and then when we've worked late and I have to be back here early."

"Does anyone else live here?"

"Drake Henson bunks out here. But he's not here right now."

She nodded her head and glanced out at the trees surrounding the front of the house.

She seemed a little nervous and he wondered if she'd ever had a boyfriend before. As pretty as she was, he highly doubted she had escaped that.

When he reached for her hand, she didn't look at him or respond. She didn't seem to know what to do. "I graduated high school last year. I feel really lucky to have landed this job. I guess you're headed into your junior year now—maybe?"

She giggled at that. "Are you kidding me. I'm...

The rattle of a diesel engine pulling up to the side of the cabin caused them both to look up and stare toward the corner of the house.

"If that's my dad—I'm dead," she whispered.

Ben wondered then if she was forbidden to visit with a boy. Maybe *he* was—dead!

Andy Parker sauntered around the corner and both Ben and Jenny let out a breath simultaneously. But the look on Andy's face was not the friendly one they were used to seeing.

"Hey, Andy." Ben got up from the swing and met him at the edge of the porch. "What's up?"

Andy glanced at Jenny who looked like she'd just been caught stealing a cookie. "Well, maybe nothing's up. At least, I hope not."

Ben half turned to look at Jenny. Then back to Andy.

"Jen, honey, how did you get all the way out here?"

"I rode Little John over."

Andy pursed his lips thoughtfully and nodded his head up and down. "Well, it's about to be dark. That's a long way to ride back in the dark. If you want to ride him back to the ranch yard," he pointed his thumb directly behind himself, "I'll drive both of you home."

She jumped up, seeming to just realize how late it was. "Okay, thank you. I'll head over there now."

"Good girl. I'll be about five minutes behind you."

After she headed toward the pen behind the house, Andy motioned for Ben to step inside the house. "Ben, this may or may not be any of my business. I'm not Jenny's dad or even kin to her for that matter—but I'm going to give you a fact or two and you can do what you want to with it."

Ben squinted his eyes, not real sure what was coming. "Okay."

"Fact number one…that little girl out there is just that…a fourteen-year-old little girl. Just between me and you, she hasn't spent five minutes away from mom and dad in her life. To my way of thinking, that's an immature fourteen." He could clearly see the shock that crossed Ben's face was genuine.

"Fourteen! I thought she was at least sixteen or…she's not even in high school."

"Fact number two should speak for itself now. Her daddy…"

Ben threw up his hand. "I get it. I get it." He shook his head. "I didn't know, Andy, and I never touched her—never kissed her—nothing—I swear to God."

"All right. Then I believe we're done here."

"Yes, sir. Plumb done!" His eyes were saucered .

Andy turned around and headed for his truck holding in the chuckles until he backed up out of sight. *You're a hero Andy Parker! You just can't tell anybody.*

A storm was coming—An early snow that was predicted to be a doozy. Mitch well remembered the last bad one from a few years back. All the highways in this part of the state were shut down for days—Beau and Carly were lost in the canyons before they married, hold up in some thief's dugout that was buried under huge snowbanks. He wasn't working here then but had heard the story more than once.

He swung open the back door of the newly built bunkhouse to enjoy the early morning cool. SaraLou came to his mind just then. He saw her most days when Ben or Drake worked in the same area he did. Strange as it seemed, that pup refused to stay with him in the new bunkhouse. She was happy sleeping in familiar surroundings in the old place with the other cowboys that came and went. Clint Berry had given her to Mitch when he and Abby moved upstate. He still claimed her as his own—making sure she had plenty of food and water out in the old place every day.

Sam, Daisy's big collie mix waddled past him slow and easy to take up his spot on the porch. His legs were stiff with age, at least sixteen or seventeen years and he slept a lot, but he was well fed and well loved.

Sam had helped save Daisy's life almost a year ago when he'd led Mitch to a closet she was held prisoner in. Nothing was too good for him as far as Mitch and Daisy were concerned. He bossed this area of the ranch most days—when he was awake.

"What do I need to do to help get us ready for this snowstorm?" She walked up behind her husband and bear-hugged him from the back. This was all new and exciting for her and Mitch wasn't about to put a damper on it. He was just going to have to get excited with her.

He turned and pulled her around to his side, giving her shoulders a tight squeeze. "I don't know how deep this might get. Weatherman is predicting several feet, so maybe you should drive into Jackson Hole and stock up on a few days' worth of goodies. It'll be tonight sometime when it comes in."

"The Brandon's and Mr. and Mrs. Walton are supposed to fly back tonight. I hope they're watching the weather situation here and not get caught where they can't get home."

"I promise you; Andy or Donny will let them know."

He reached for his hat and wrapped the same arm around her neck, pulling her in for a long, slow kiss. When he raised his head, his smile matched the warmth of his kiss all the way into the depth of his smoky blues. "I better get saddled up before I change my mind. This is going to be a long day. Get your shopping done first thing this morning, please."

"I will."

After she saw him ride off and out of sight, she headed for the woodpile behind the two-stall barn that was built to match the log bunkhouse. A few times after riding one of the ranch geldings late in the evening, Mitch let her stall him in this barn and ride him back to headquarters the next day. She would never say it out loud, but to have a horse out the back door in this little barn that belonged to her would be almost too much to dream for.

She could never ask for more than what she had here. It was incredible the life she was now living. High Point Dude Ranch was her home—she was married to the most handsome, loving man she'd ever known—a cowboy who truly loved her. He had taken her on with all her flaws and faults—nightmares with screams or moans, fighting the air that was teaming with invisible monsters yanking her hair and kicking her. When she suddenly awakened from it, she was always wrapped in Mitch's strong, loving arms. Thinking about it now, she realized for the first time that she hadn't had a bad dream in a while. She couldn't actually remember the last one.

Smiling with happy thankfulness, she grasped the handles of the wheelbarrow that set beside the barn and pushed it around the back side to Mitch's *six-pack pile* as he referred to his wood chopping. He generally spent an hour or two every day splitting logs to fit their fireplace and whoever else needed wood.

She had seen him look at the log rack on the back porch late last night after learning about the coming winter storm. Even though the cabin had electric heat, they both enjoyed a roaring fire on cold evenings.

It took several heavy loads to fill the rack and her best bud, Sam, made every step alongside her before stretching out on the back porch for a snooze.

She grabbed her purse and keys from the house and headed for her car feeling proud of herself for thinking to get wood hauled to the cabin.

It wasn't that she didn't know how to work or that she'd done without necessities or luxuries growing up. She was as normal as any in that respect. But she had lost a lot of ability to think for herself—to see what needed to be done—take hold and do it. She'd been denied the privilege of growing into who she was meant to be.

Daisy's mom was a controller. More than that—a complete narcissist whose interest in life consisted of only herself—to the destruction of anyone who stepped out of agreement with her opinions—even and especially of those of her own household. A sociopathic narcissist was the diagnosis on her chart at the mental institution that a judge had ordered her taken to a year ago.

Daisy was raised by this woman in such a way that she had demanded and succeeded in gaining control of her mind—her soul. She had been only allowed to do what she was ordered to do and a negative expression on her face in the process got her bruised. She learned early on to keep a straight, zombie-like face, no matter what happened to or around her—which grievously followed her into her adult life. She left her mother's house at age eighteen, with no idea how to navigate daily life.

She managed to work and acquired a small apartment, where she had mysteriously found a name and phone number scribbled on a scrap of paper in the mailbox of her apartment. Ridiculously compelled, she called the number that turned out to be a Christian counselor.

After a short conversation with the young girl on the line, the counselor set up pro-bono sessions with her that lasted for a few months.

Daisy had no idea who put *that* information in *that* mailbox, but it became her salvation—a huge step in learning how to become a whole person—to think—to feel—to desire to live and love like a normal, independent human being.

The fact that both of her siblings had died during their teen years due to their inability to cope with the trauma of their raising was the one aspect of her life she had never been able to accept nor talk about. She'd been cruelly robbed of her sister and brother and she only hoped someday to find a true place of forgiveness in her heart for the perpetrator of that.

When she went out the door of the cabin, it was apparent that the weather was already changing. The wind had picked up and it was definitely colder. She couldn't help but feel excited about the coming snow.

She kept her thoughts on the day at hand, rejecting every past heart-stabbing memory that popped into her head. *No,* she would repeat aloud until it left and she'd immediately replay the thought with a happy one. And that wasn't so hard to do these days.

Within an hour and a half, she was headed back home with enough groceries for a month. Heavy clouds had moved in, darkening the skies.

A couple miles out of town, Daisy caught sight of a furry little spotted animal a short distance in front of her on the side of the road, close to the fence line. Her first thought was a *fawn* bedded down in the thin spindly weeds that barely concealed it. But, when she drove by, she realized it was a small dog that intently watched her car pass.

With nothing in sight but wide-open space, she knew the little pup needed help. How had it gotten all the way out here—and with this freezing storm about to hit.

She pulled off the two-lane highway into the grass far enough to make a quick U-turn. She crossed over a concrete culvert which she didn't notice from the other direction and slowed to a stop. The dog stood, it's eyes pleading, tail wagging. She squatted down and put a handout toward it.

"Come on, sweetie. You can go home with me."

The little spaniel crept warily toward her, desperately wanting to trust the outstretched hand. It stopped and looked up into Daisy's face, then squirmed and wiggled toward her again almost sliding its belly on the ground. The humbled and fearful little dog was breaking Daisy's heart. Those huge round eyes were begging this human to be kind.

When the cold wet nose was close enough to touch her fingertips, Daisy could finally see that *it* was a female and appeared to be pregnant. She patted her head, then scooped her up and carried her to the car. Afraid of making her sick, she opted to not give her food—only a few licks of water from the palm of her hand until reaching home. She lay in the front passenger seat and slept soundly until Daisy turned the car motor off beside the bunkhouse.

Once inside, she ate heartily and lapped a cup of warm milk, then curled in the corner close to her food bowl and slept.

Daisy unloaded and put up the groceries, then busied herself with laundry and fresh flannel bed linens and extra quilts on their king bed.

The pup seemed extra nervous toward late afternoon. Daisy let her outside and she seemed even more restless—whimpering and frantically sniffing the ground around the yard.

It had gotten colder and darker.

The sound of Mitch's truck coming in scared her and she ran to hover between Daisy's feet. She picked her up and carried her out to meet him.

"Hey—what have you got there?" Mitch grinned and kissed his bride.

"She was sitting on the side of the highway when I headed back from town. I think someone must have dumped her. She's slept all day but has gotten really nervous the past hour."

He scratched behind her ear and ran a hand down her back, then took her from Daisy. His hand became wet and sticky and he looked under her belly. "Daise, this girl has recently had puppies. She's got milk but doesn't appear to have been nursed much."

"Oh," her hand was wet, too. "I only saw *her*. But—I didn't look around. I had no idea."

"This is not a young dog. Anything could have happened to them." He examined her stomach and sides again. "She definitely has already had them."

"It's going to freeze. We have to go back and look for them…just in case."

"Do you recall the exact spot you picked her up?"

She looked off to visualize the place. "Yes…she was close to a concrete culvert that ran underneath the highway."

"I know right where it is. Let's load up and go look before it gets dark…"

Daisy ran in and let Samson in at the back door. The back porch was his favorite place to lounge and sleep, but she insisted he come inside at dark. Then she loaded up with Mitch and the pup.

Minutes later, he pulled off the road just past the culvert. It had begun to lightly snow as he set the mama dog down near the underground drain. Immediately she disappeared down the embankment and inside where Mitch and Daisy followed with a flashlight.

And there they were—two little furry spotted newborns—cold and hungry.

Mitch could just reach them without having to crawl more than a couple feet inside. Handing them off to Daise, he searched around, then scooped up mama dog and quickly headed back. Snow was falling thick and fast as they reached home.

The new family was bedded down on a blanket in a warm corner of the kitchen—mama dog being a good mama, settled in with her brood of two.

Samson showed no excitement about it all but lay down just off the blanket beside the group as a self-appointed guardian.

Mitch and Daisy watched the snow blow through from the front porch until the cold ran both of them back inside. They had eaten leftover beef stew earlier, that Daisy had made the day before, and the kitchen cleaned up.

She checked on the pups one last time while Mitch headed for the shower—finding them all, including Sam, sound asleep.

After her quick shower, she turned off the lights and slid under the heavy quilts beside her man. He pulled her against him and draped a leg across hers when he felt her shivering.

"You're freezing. Maybe I should have built a fire."

"No, the electric heaters are enough. I just ran out of hot water before I got all the soap off. I'll warm up in a minute."

"I did notice that you filled the wood rack. I appreciate that. It must have taken you several trips."

"Oh—I had help. Samson made every step I did." She smoothed her fingers across his spiky, unshaved cheek. "I just wanted to do something worthwhile to help you. You work so hard for us."

He grasped her hand and brought it to his lips, kissing her palm, then her fingers. "*Something worthwhile*—and you're not joking one bit, are you? You really don't have a clue what you do for me every day—and night."

"What do you mean?"

He chuckled. "*That* is what I mean right there. You don't know. You get up and cook my breakfast every morning, you keep my clothes clean and this cabin is spotless. You've made flower beds and a vegetable garden last spring. I have to force the issue of us eating at headquarters from the chuck wagon, so you don't have to cook and clean in the evenings. You're always upbeat and smiling and so contented with this life we have. And—you're always so ready and willing to make love—morning, noon or midnight. *That's* what I mean."

She was quiet, trying to digest what he'd just said about her—trying to feel about herself the same way he did.

He knew she couldn't believe much good about herself. "You know what, baby girl? The day *will* come when you'll finally recognize your worth. For now, you'll just have to let me recognize it for you."

He raised up on his forearm and pulled her almost beneath him as he licked his lips and bent his head to lay a warm, sensual, wet kiss on her lips that she eagerly accepted. She liked the feel of the rough stubble on his jaw. She liked him clean shaved. She liked him covered in dust and sweat—or showered and dressed up or down or not at all. This man was the hero she so desperately needed and she would be the woman he needed in every way she knew and could learn how.

She was aware of how exhausted he was tonight. "Goodnight, Mitch. Get some rest," she whispered.

When he eased back to his pillow, he pulled her against him, curling around her in a perfect fit. Within seconds—he was asleep. She followed suite minutes later.

Earlier that day
California

Karlotta took a long minute to gather her thoughts. She stared at the headstone—remembering—so she could gather her courage before she began her story.

"When I was a little girl, about five years old, I had a very strange dream one night. I remember it clearly to this day. A beautiful lady came into my bedroom and leaned down over me speaking many things into my ear, but I couldn't remember anything she said after I awakened the next morning. I told my father about the lady in the dream and he laughed and said he wished he had such pleasant dreams."

"My family were all very religious in the sense of attending Christian Mass on Sundays. During other times, they did bad things to people. They hurt them or killed them. I know this only because I heard conversation when no one knew I was around. They gave a lot of money to the church in exchange for forgiveness. I was confused by this and one day I questioned my father about something I had seen and heard. I was seventeen years old and soon after that, he forced me to be married to one of his bad men, to keep me in line and never eavesdrop or question what I knew. Asa Montoya was older but treated me well enough. But...I made a terrible mistake when I confided my most precious secret to him. It was after you killed my young brother," she glanced up at Hank, then back down, "and I was grieving with the rest of my family. I knew things...about being dead and...leaving this world. I wanted to talk about it to try to help the grief, especially my father's. It had been almost a year. During this time, I had secretly purchased a beautiful headstone for your parents and placed flowers there. After confiding to my husband about the granite marker and the flowers...and why I did it...the next morning a doctor came and gave me an injection. When I awakened later that day, I thought I was in a hospital, but it was the asylum for the insane. I had been committed there and left for a very long time."

At this point, Hank stepped over to her and sat beside her on the bench. She didn't respond but continued staring at the Rhea's grave. She was quiet for a time. No one else moved a muscle—just waited for her to say all that she needed to.

"One day, I was given some clothes that could be worn on the outside of the asylum and was then driven to the home I had been taken from many years before. I soon learned that my husband and father were dead. Others of my family were dead as well. Only Sara, the woman who helped my father raise me was there. She was always in the background when I was growing up. She was very fearful. My mother died when I was born—I was told. Sara was responsible for getting me released. She gave me quite a large sum of money and I left." She was quiet for a few moments. "I've never spoken of my secret since I told Asa Montoya that night. But now I will tell you, because that will answer your question of how I know you were coming here. I prayed very hard and often for you and for your family's peace. During my prayers—God began to speak to me. I could feel His Presence and His Thoughts would come into my mind. He would tell me wonderful things about His Heaven and answer my questions. When I was in so much pain because of your family, I asked God what could I do and He said to honor their memory with a marker and pretty flowers. He said your mother liked flowers. I did this every week for them to be remembered."

She looked up at Hank, tears glistening in her tired, red-rimmed eyes and took his hand in hers. "Mr. Rhea…God told me this morning you would come here today. I wanted so badly to tell you how sorry I am for this horrible thing My family did. I asked God many years ago for this chance before I die. And very soon I will go to my Jesus. He answered my greatest desire. I am so very very sorry."

Hank very gently put both arms around her fragile little body and hugged her while both of them cried.

Laura and Martha wiped drips off their cheeks again and again. Jesse had squatted beside Laura's side of the bench and ran his fingers back and forth across his face.

After a couple of minutes when everyone pulled their emotions together, Laura stood and went to the woman who was now standing.

"Karlotta, I'm Laura Brandon." She waved a hand toward the man just behind her. "This is my husband, Jesse and I'd like you to meet …Buck's wife, Martha." Each responded to the introductions. "This is the most incredible story and I'm so glad you felt you could share it. I need to tell *you* something now."

The woman's full attention was on Laura's face—eagerly staring into her eyes.

"The Lord just showed me that you believe you were hidden away in the asylum because your father was afraid you knew too much."

"Yes. I know a lot of his evil dealings with people and he found out that I knew he was responsible for the murder of these sweet people." She nodded toward the Rhea's plots.

"The Lord said your father feared God's calling on your life—a call to be close and intimate with Him where you learned to hear his Voice and he feared your willingness to be obedient to whatever God asked of you. But He used you in a great way inside the walls of the asylum. You did good work for Him while there—causing many patients to be in Heaven today. It was a hard task that He gave you, but He says—*Daughter, Great Is Your Reward In Heaven.*"

The elderly woman's eyes grew as she touched her fingers to her lips in shock. "You hear Him speak, too! Oh—bless you, dear Laura.

You could not have known these things." She reached an arm around Laura and hugged her.

After a few more minutes, the group said their good-byes. Karlotta refused a ride back to her apartment as she used this walk each week for needed exercise.

The foursome all knew they would never see her again, but after this past hour listening to a story that can't be made up—each knew their lives would not feel the same again. Something like this has a way of changing the way you think and respond to the people in your world that you love. You want to hold them a little longer and tighter, kiss that special one more passionately, play ball or hide-n-seek with more enthusiasm and laughter.

Hank spent a little more time beside his folk's graves while the others waited in the car. He was fully aware that his family were not in these graves but had been living well in Heaven since the moment of their deaths. But this stone with their names seemed to help him connect with a life he could barely remember. Oh—he remembered in detail—Buck Rhea's details, but the bond he had with that life wasn't there now. And that was a blessing. He'd said his good-byes decades ago. His mama and daddy were living in God's World and when his time came, the Rhea family would all come full circle.

For now, he was Hank Walton. His world was Highpoint Dude Ranch with his woman and all the kids—old ones and young ones who loved and depended on their Gramps and Granny. That's where his heart was. It took this trip to give him a real release—to know fully that God had everything taken care of.

He headed toward the car and watched his wife step out and walk to meet him. She moved into his arms and he grinned down at her and squeezed her in a long hug. "Granny girl, let's go home to our family."

***

CHAPTER FIVE

The Wyoming-bound travelers managed to be on one of the last flights to get clearance to land at Jackson airport. Granny Martha was a loony-tune by the time the jet touched down. She hadn't looked out the window even once but was fully aware of the storm raging as the plane rocked and dipped.

The pilot stood at the exit ramp apologizing profusely for the bumpy ride. When he saw Martha's pale face as she went out, he followed to make sure she would be all right.

The sight of Donny and Andy standing in the waiting area was all she needed to get her grip back—them and a few sips of strong, black coffee. They both hugged her and Andy told her he'd seen angels beneath the plane holding it steady earlier that day when he prayed for them. "I knew you would all make it home just fine."

"I guess everything's good at home?" Jesse asked.

"Yes, sir," Andy answered, "all is snug as a bug. We brought tire chains. Didn't figure you had any in the truck."

"I appreciate that. Hadn't thought about it yet. I'll get them put on if you want to help Mom get our bags."

"You're ready to roll, Dad. Soon as Granny's up to it, I'll follow you. This storm is going to get worse before it's over."

"I'll drive for you, brother. I'm all practiced up."

Jesse nodded and gave Donny's back a pat.

Hank kept a hold on Martha until they were safely in Andy's warm dually.

Jesse and Laura retrieved the two bags and loaded up with chauffer-Donny.

An hour and a half later, Andy tracked to his house and picked up Granny Martha's aged little dog, Bonny. Emma Jo acted as caregiver for her while Granny was gone.

Anna Leigh and Jesse Dane, Jr were already home after spending the night with their Uncle Donny and Aunt Reeny. Little five-year-old, Donny Hank, was overjoyed at having his *big kid* cousins stay overnight at his house. They returned home early in the afternoon and cleaned the house, as a welcome home surprise for their parents, before helping get the petting zoo animals bedded down inside the barn and haul in and stack extra bales of hay for the horses. These Brandon kids were well used to hard work on their family ranch. But they played every bit as hard as they worked.

By midnight, the snow was blowing and several feet deep in low areas. All were home and safe. Jesse returned Judd Luke's call to let them know they were all home before sliding into bed beside his wife.

Neither spoke a word for a while but lay on their backs staring into the darkness. He reached for her hand and entwined his fingers in hers, unable to shut down his thoughts. It had been a solemn trip home and still finding words—even trivial conversation, was just not there. Had they not taken this trip, they would never have known Karlotta Montoya ever existed or what she had gone through during her life because of someone else's evil choices. She'd done nothing wrong yet paid dearly because her father did. Where was the justice in that?

Laura felt his hand and arm stiffen slightly. She cut her eyes toward him. "What are you thinking about?"

"How unfair life is for some people. For others—it seems like happiness is fairly easy to come by. I've stood back and observed the laughter and happiness from everyone on this ranch and on the Double OO. We've all had our ups and downs—some traumatic events here and there—but then there's Ms. Karlotta." He was silent for a long time before continuing. "Her entire adult life has been filled with pain and sorrow. Today—she's a lonely old lady. Apparently, she's going to finish her life like that...and Laura, ...*she loves God!* She hears His Voice...like you do."

She could hear the stressed tone of his voice, bordering on anger now. Confusion. And she understood exactly what he was saying. She had been pondering this same thing ever since they drove out of the cemetery early that day. The things God allows to happen in some of our lives—situations that seem the purest of evil—HE always has a Good Purpose in letting one of HIS children, like Karlotta, go through the fire of trials while another seems to escape the worst of it.

She turned on her side to face him and smoothed her hand down the front of his T-shirt. "I think, honey, we just have to be content with letting God be God to each of us. We don't know anything about Mrs. Montoya other than what she chose to tell us. All we can do is be the best we can be in the place God chose to put us."

After a silent moment, Jesse said, "I think we should say a prayer together for her right now."

They both prayed whatever came to mind, first Jesse, then Laura—before holding each other a little tighter than usual to finally fall asleep.

Mitch jerked his head up off the pillow, then raised halfway to a sitting position. The room was pitch dark—he jerked the towel off the lighted digital clock on his bedside lamp table. It was 2:46 AM. He hit the floor and hurried out of the bedroom, heading to the front door, certain he'd been awakened by someone banging on it. But it was the back door that was standing wide open with blizzard-like cold air pouring in. Apparently, it didn't get locked or even closed all the way. It was a sturdy, well-built door.

He flipped on the kitchen light to find mama dog and babies snuggled up, but Samson was gone. If he wasn't in the bedroom, he probably went outside for a potty run while the door was open.

The cold had penetrated his sweats and T-shirt and he hurried back to the bedroom certain he'd find Sam curled on the rug on Daisy's side. A quick flip of the light revealed that not only was old Samson not in the room, but neither was Daisy.

He stepped into the hallway. The bathroom light was off and the door was open. *What the...?*

"Daisy?!"

No answer.

The cabin was small and it was obvious that neither Daisy nor her dog were in it. He wheeled around toward the kitchen, then nearly tripped over himself as he wheeled again on second thought toward the bedroom to step into his boots. Five seconds later, he snatched the long handled, heavy duty flashlight off the kitchen counter and raced outside. The snow had stopped falling, but at least two foot had come down.

"Daisy!" He jumped off the porch into the drift that was above his knees. "Daisy! Answer me!"

She'd left an easy trail in the deep powder. He ran in her steps, shining the light as far ahead as it would go—straight toward the woodpile behind the small barn.

"Oh, Lord God!" His words were a prayer when the light fell on her bright pink sweats that covered her legs and on her small bare feet. The rest of her was hidden beneath Sam's thick winter fur. The dog was curled on top of her, keeping her warm.

"Daise? Baby?" He reached behind Sam to urge him to get up off her. "Get up, Samson. Come on, old man. Good boy." Mitch helped the dog get onto his rickety legs, then reached for Daisy's arms and sat her up enough to get her secured in his arms. She hadn't been out here long, thank God, but she was shaking. He carried her easily back to the house, not sure she was awake. She hadn't uttered a sound.

When he reached the bedroom, she raised her head to look around. "Mitch, where are you taking me? It's freezing in here."

He stood her on the floor. "Daisy, do you know you were outside asleep in the snow?"

She shook her head and looked confused, beginning to shake harder.

"Get those clothes off—they're wet." He stepped to their dresser and pulled a clean dry pair of sweats out of her drawer and a white long sleeve V-neck T-shirt. He didn't have to tell her twice to change clothes. Her teeth were chattering when he got her under the mound of quilts on the bed.

"I'll be back in two minutes." He pointed the electric heater toward her side of the bed and closed the door behind him as he left to lock up and check on Sam.

He found Daisy's furry guardian curled beside mama dog's bed. "I owe you, buddy. Thank you." He ran his hands over Sam, then gave mama dog a pat on her head—slid the dead bolt on the back door, then the front door, and changed his clothes and slid in beside Daisy.

She had lain there waiting for him, confused and afraid of what had taken place. She knew she'd had a nightmare, but—what else happened?

His strong arm encircled her waist to drag her backward, snugly into his protective curve. Now that he had a moment to consider what had happened tonight, he couldn't keep from pulling her tighter against him.

"Mitch," she whispered so low, he could barely hear her, "what happened? Why were you carrying me?"

He stilled inside. She didn't know she'd ever left the house. She had no clue how close she came to dying tonight—freezing to death. What if he hadn't heard the door bang open—woke up enough to get up and investigate?

"Daise…have you ever suddenly found yourself in a room of your home or outside and didn't really remember going there—wondered how you got in that place?"

She was quiet for a while before finally answering him in a whisper. "Yes. A couple of times."

"Tonight, you walked outside and laid down against the back of the barn…by the woodpile in the snow. Sam went with you and was laying on top of you. I heard the door banging really loud against the wall. It woke me up. Did you have another nightmare?"

"I remember something was chasing me. I ran and ran, but it grabbed my hair and slammed me to the ground."

"Then what?"

"Then you were carrying me in here…all wet and cold."

He ran a hand through her partially damp hair, smoothing it back from her face, then kissed the back of her head. "You were sleepwalking with a bad dream. But you're safe now. Let's get some sleep. We'll talk more tomorrow."

He was shaken with worry concerning this new revelation about his little bride but fought through it by asking the Lord to give her restful sleep and keeping her safe the remainder of the night.

Soon her breathing became calm and even and they both slept.

By 8 AM the next morning, the sun was glaring off of the fresh white ground—Thankfully the early winter storm bumped into a high-pressure system that pushed it more eastward.

The three amigos—also known as, Summer, Emma Jo and Rachel were bundled up and a little impatiently waiting for Andy to *unsuspectingly* emerge from the back door and head for the barn. Armed to the teeth with well-formed snowballs, the trio heard him at the door where he always put his boots on and then headed out. Any second now!

Summer put a finger to her mouth reminding them to be quiet, then pointed at the back door. Hands were loaded with ammo.

The squealing from the three unsuspecting bombers could be heard all across the ranch when Andy snuck in behind them and crowned all three of them with a huge block of snow he'd carefully lifted off the hood of his dually.

"Oh, dude, that was so mean. You've had it now, mister!"
Summer was giggling so hard; she could hardly give the order to her little army to begin firing.

"Yeah, Andy, you done it now…mister." Emma Jo had a pitcher's arm on her little seven-year-old frame and busted him right between the eyes.

He chased her and tackled her, almost losing sight of her in the deep snow drift that had banked up against the back of the house. When he grasped her arm and pulled her out, she came up with another snowball, landing it in his mouth. More ammo and bodies pounced from behind landing him face first in the deep drift. He raised up spitting snow, yelling in full surrender— "Ya'll killing me! I give up. I give up!"

It took a few seconds before five-year-old Rachel's voice was heard and discerned to be in real distress. "No, Daddy! Don't be killed!" She was crying and screaming—fear crinkling her little face as she threw herself into Andy's arms and wrapped her arms around his neck.

Everyone stopped and stared for a couple seconds while what they'd all heard sank in. Rachel had just called Andy, *Daddy*. He'd always been *Andy* to both girls by their own choice. Rachel simply followed whatever Emma Jo did.

Summer reached for her, but Andy put up a hand to stop her. He was taken aback at the sound of *Daddy* coming from her and her reaction to his playful remark about killing him.

He tightened his hold on her with both arms wrapped around her. "Rach, baby, I'm all right. I was just playing." He paused a moment. "Daddy's not going anywhere." *Lord, he loved the sound of that!* *Daddy.*

She raised up and looked into his eyes, her face wet with streaming tears. "You promise?"

"Yes, I promise. And you know what else?"

She scrubbed her eyes with her gloved fists and shook her head.

"I really like that you called me Daddy."

"Be...because that's your real name?"

"That's right, baby. My name is Daddy."

Emma Jo took a step closer to Andy. "I want to call you Daddy, too."

"Thank you, Em. That makes me really happy."

Summer wiped tears off her cheeks and chuckled as she and Andy exchanged glances.

"Let's go inside and celebrate how happy we are today with some hot chocolate." Andy grasped Summer's outstretched hand to let her help pull him up out of the snow.

"I'll get the marshmallows," cried Emma Jo, as both girls disappeared inside.

Andy and Summer stood for a moment and exchanged a look of love and intimacy that only they could understand. His chin quivered at the idea of his new position with their girls—one that he wouldn't take a million bucks for.

He opened the door for Summer to go inside and made a mental note to petition his Heavenly Father for a long life—long enough to get Rachel raised up. After all—he promised.

Judd Luke backed his dually out of the carport and headed toward the main road with Jenny so she could catch the school bus.

It was just breaking daylight with a long day ahead helping the hands separate calves from their mama's and a group of heifers without calves to haul to the sale. It was never pleasant listening to the bawling cows and calves and he'd seriously thought about leaving the job to his cowboys. He guessed he was just getting too old for this job but knew it had more to do with Toni carrying another baby for him. He understood even more today how she had felt the day they rode out and found two heifers bawling over their dead calves.

When he'd left the house this morning, Toni was in the bathroom with her first bout of morning sickness after smelling fresh coffee dripping. He didn't want to leave her like that, but Jenny had to get to school and he had to man up and go hear the cows cry. His eyes began to burn and he mentally kicked his own butt and pulled his hat brim lower on his forehead. Maybe he *was* getting too old for this.

Just as he parked on the opposite side of the road where she would board the bus, he watched a late model red BMW hesitatingly turn and drive through the ranch gate. The driver seemed lost and unsure—He couldn't tell if it was a male or female, but the Texas tagged car headed toward the house.

Julie had only been here once, but that was many years ago for her best friend's wedding. The scenery looked different, but she recognized enough to feel sure she was in the right place. She knew she should have tried to call before coming but being foot loose and basically passing through the state to—nowhere in particular—she could chance a quick surprise visit.

The last time she spoke to Toni was just before her spur-of-the-minute Las Vegas wedding and her life had spiraled into a pit of hell since that day. And that was only her *first* husband. She had thought of her friend many times through the years, but what could she talk about if she called her. Even this drive through the upper states and heading up this driveway today was an unplanned trip. She got into her car with all that she owned and started driving. And here she stood on Toni Barton Luke's porch, pressing the doorbell.

It didn't occur to Toni that anyone would be at the door other than her husband. It was too early for anyone else. He probably locked himself out of the back door.

With her hair sticking out in eight different directions and her face looking like it had just puked, she swung open the door. Her eyes saucered, giving her a family resemblance to Beetle Juice himself.

It took Julie a few seconds to find her voice. "Oh my God! And to think I was just feeling sorry for myself a few seconds ago. Girl…my cat, if I had one, wouldn't even drag you in!"

"Julie!" Toni reached her arms out, but suddenly stepped back, "Oh…" slapped her hand over her mouth, grabbed her stomach and ran for the bathroom.

Julie stepped inside and waited a couple minutes before moving to sit in the high-backed chair at the foot of the stairs. It didn't appear that anyone else was home. The log house was still as beautiful as she remembered, just a little more lived in. Homey.

She heard the backdoor open, then close and she stood up and leaned forward toward that direction. "Hello?"

The face that entered the room was only slightly recognizable. It was an older, fuller face than she remembered. "Judd?"

"Yes, mam, I am. Have we met?" He removed his Stetson and shook her hand.

"Yes, but it was brief and a long time ago. Julie Langston."

The name instantly widened his eyes and brought a smile. "Julie—Toni's friend and maid of honor from Texas. It sure has been a while." He looked across the den toward the hallway. "I'm guessing Toni knows you're here."

"She was here long enough to let me in but was about to be sick and went that way." She pointed her finger. "I was thinking I should go see about her.'

"I will. Excuse me a minute." He strode off hurriedly toward their bed and bath area.

Not sure what to do, she went into the kitchen and found a half pot of coffee. Finding a mug in the cabinet, she filled it and sat back down in the same chair. She was getting worried now, not knowing why Toni was so sick. Maybe she should just go—but not before knowing what was wrong.

She took in the interior of the house, as much of it as she could see. The gray and turquoise tile floor was rich—the red rock fireplace with a long, wide slab of rustic shaped cedar for a mantle. The top of the mantle held several framed pictures. She got up and crossed the den so she could get close enough to see who was in the pics. A family portrait of Judd and Toni with two young girls graced the center of the shelf with smaller pictures of the two girls when they were younger. These were Toni's daughters. She'd been very pregnant with the oldest when she and Judd had their wedding—although they had been *legally* married almost a year before. The other girl was obviously a second daughter. Then several photos of a little boy and a wedding picture of the oldest girl with her groom and the little boy.

She stepped back and slowly shook her head. It had been a whole family ago since she and Toni were friends. Toni had this to show for all these years gone by and she had nothing except welts and bruises and—money. She had plenty of that—and she'd had a fancier home in some respects than this one—but it was cold and spotlessly unlivable.

She thought momentarily about her first husband Robert. He was so much fun—wined and dined her, promising her world travels and parties. After an evening of drinking and gambling in Las Vegas, they got married in a cute little wedding chapel. Two months later, he left her a note on *her* apartment kitchen table where they lived in Dallas, to say he wouldn't be back—and she had been okay with that. They were never in love with each other.

Then there was Mark. They met on a Caribbean cruise ship—her first vacation traveling on water, and he fell for her the first time they'd laid eyes on each other. The captain of the ship married them. So romantic. He was *beautiful* to look at—Greek-God style—a true gentleman—*And he* was filthy rich. A beautiful, Greek-God, very rich gentleman. That was Mark. And she soon learned how well his name fit him. He left his *mark* on her almost daily in stinging slaps, deep bruises, twisted, swollen wrists and even a broken collar bone when he'd slammed her against the wall.

Intimidated and bullied, she couldn't find a way out. Pure fear had gripped her mind by his threats of worse torture if she ever left him—until a couple months ago. Mark was dead—killed instantly in a head-on collision about a mile from their two-story mansion.

She had felt nothing but relief when the police knocked on her door with the news. And she felt nothing when his lawyers, or whoever they were, came to the house to inform her that his will provided nothing for her except an acceptable bank account and her car, so she could feel free to pack and leave immediately. She left within a couple days and rented a suite in the Waldorf until she could figure out where she wanted to go. She let the worst of the *marks* heal up before checking out of the suite and hitting the road.

Standing here now in this family's home of obvious normalcy, she suddenly realized she didn't belong in this world. What did she have to share with her childhood best friend? That time was gone. They weren't kids anymore and all she could offer Toni or her lovely family in these pictures was something from the darker side of bad choices in her life.

After returning the coffee mug to the kitchen sink, she headed for the front door. The moment she pulled it open, intending to rush out and disappear, the doorbell rang and she nearly plowed into a cowboy who was decked out like an old west wrangler. His leather gloved hand closed over her arm to steady her and stop her forward momentum.

"Oh...I'm so sorry. Forgive me." Once she got past the shock, she laughed up at him.

His eyes grew and he smiled as he reached up and removed his old, battered straw Stetson—not realizing he was still gripping her arm. His spurs jangled when he shifted his weight to the opposite leg—his weight was all in his height of about six foot three or four.

Julie knew she was staring up into his face too long, but those blue eyes were the gentlest and kindest she'd ever seen. There was something genuine about what she saw and she was mesmerized. He was roughly handsome, straight white teeth and graying around his temples—and so kind.

Finally, he released her arm and broke the spell that had captured them for a few moments. "I'm AJ Call, mam." He offered her his hand.

She shook hands noticing how his long, thin fingers swallowed hers. "Julie Langston."

He squinted at her, a crease forming between his eyes. "Ms. Julie...forgive me for staring, but you look a little familiar to me. Have we met before?"

"I don't know. I was only here once...on Judd and Toni's wedding day."

He grinned broadly then. "Well, it's been a few years for sure, but I remember you. I surely do. You stood up with Toni in the ceremony."

Surprised, she smiled broadly, "Yes, I did. Thank you for...remembering."

"Julie! Oh my word, I'm so sorry." Toni came from the hallway looking refreshed and not a bit older than Julie remembered. She'd put on a little makeup and her hair in a ponytail. Judd was right on her heels. She threw her arms around her oldest and dearest friend. "It's been so long, Julie. You look great! I can't believe you're standing here."

Judd stepped past the women and pushed the door open wider. "Come on in, AJ. We're having a surprise hen party."

He chuckled. "So, I see. Ms. Julie and I were just renewing our acquaintance from yours and Toni's wedding day. But I won't intrude. I'm headed to the ninety and was hoping you had an extra key to the supply house. Somebody forgot to put it back or maybe locked it up inside the building."

"Got one in my dually." He glanced at the women. They'd retreated into the den, chattering like magpies—He and AJ went to work.

"Julie, I can't believe how much you've changed. You're more beautiful than ever—long blonde hair, so slim and trim. I want to know what's going on in your life."

"I'm just doing a little traveling…seeing the sights. But I noticed the pictures on your mantel. I'd love to hear about your family."

Toni was quick to recognize how she turned the conversation away from herself. The torment she could see in her beautiful green eyes was heartbreaking. Julie's smile was beautiful, but her mouth is as far as it went.

For the next hour, Toni filled her in on the past twenty years at the Double OO and the Luke household. "And to finish off the story, Abby is giving us another grand baby next April."

"Well, I'm genuinely happy for you, girl. When luck fell on you, it meant business."

Toni's gaze studied her friend a few seconds. "Luck had nothing to do with it. But…enough about me. It's your turn. You went back to Dallas after my wedding…and then…?" She wiggled her eyebrows.

"Okay…so I went to Las Vegas one wild weekend, met a guy, got married…"

"What!"

"It didn't work out…got divorced, the end."

Both women stared at each other in silence a moment.

"I'm waiting."

Julie smiled faintly, "For what?"

"The rest of your twenty years. Come on…you left out something. You can't lie to me. I'm Toni."

Julie's eyes misted and she looked away.

Toni nodded her head. "Would you like some coffee?"

"I had some, thanks."

"Okay." She waited. "Jules…this is a safe place if you want to talk."

She looked up and her chin crinkled at the compassionate expression in Toni's eyes. How could she talk inside this house about the shameful life she'd lived these past few years? This place had a soft, fresh air feel to it. It was a joyful place—Everything about *her* was darkness.

Toni could see the struggle she was having, feeling she was about to bolt to the door any second. "Julie…if you hadn't come to see me today, I would not know the difference…whether your life was a good one or not. But you did come and I'm so happy you're here, but if you go without letting me help you someway, I'll worry endlessly about you."

After several minutes, she finally conceded—dropping all her defenses and held Toni's gaze as she, without emotion, told her what she had never told anyone else.

"I don't know why I couldn't leave. I didn't have any children to protect. When an officer came to my door and told me Mark was dead…I felt blank. I didn't care. I was glad…and relieved."

They sat without a word—Toni, letting the horror story she'd just heard sink in and Julie, feeling calm and knowing it didn't matter one bit that she'd told someone. He couldn't come out of that box in the ground and hurt her anymore.

"It's okay that you were glad. I'm glad about it, too."

Julie nodded her head, then gave her a quizzical look. "Why were you so sick earlier? You seem fine now."

"Morning sickness. This grandma is pregnant again."

"Toni!" She jumped up and gave her a tight hug. "How exciting for you and Cowboy. So…how old is Jenny?"

She laughed. "Nearly fifteen."

"Wow, girl…was this planned or…?"

"A slip up? We certainly did not plan it, but we're about to get used to the idea. I'm getting excited about fixing up the nursery again. Abby didn't marry until little David was a year old, so there's already a start with a few things she did…like curtains and soft yellow painted walls."

"That sounds like fun to me."

"Well…then you need to hang out here for a while and help me pick out furniture and stuff. Say you will."

"No…because I wasn't invited to be here today. I crashed your…"

"I just invited you, you silly goose, and I know you have nowhere to go and no home to go back to and I won't take no for an answer. It's beautiful here in the fall and you and I can get some serious trail riding in."

"I assume you mean on horseback?"

"Of course."

"Toni, I haven't been on a horse since we were kids and you're pregnant, remember?"

"I rode with the other two in my belly and you're out of excuses, so it's settled."

Julie laughed with a joy she hadn't felt in…ever. "Okay, but only a day or two."

"Yes!"

***

CHAPTER SIX

From the moment she'd agreed to stay at the ranch, Julie felt a peacefulness in her mind that was obvious and surprising. There was a freshness here—maybe it was the people she was with, but just the air around her felt soft—easy to breathe. She'd never experienced anything remotely similar, but she liked it.

Toni had experienced a second bout of extreme nausea that afternoon and spent most of the rest of the day in bed.

Julie had helped her fix lunch before she began feeling sick again; so, she was familiar enough with the kitchen to clean up and load the dishwasher.

After unloading a few things from her car and hauling them upstairs to the guest room, she went for a walk. The barn was a little far out from the house, but she'd been thinking seriously about needing to exercise. A walk out there would be a good start and she'd love to see some horses.

By the time she reached the barn, she was winded. Her depressed, couch potato lifestyle was showing itself for what it was—She was way too short of breath.

"Julie, you are such a wimp," she chided herself and grabbed the hay bale that was setting in front of an unoccupied horse stall, to sit down. "Turn forty and you fall to pieces." And then there's Toni—over forty and pregnant with her third child, she mused silently. She had missed it—somehow. *Life.* That's what it felt like she'd missed. She knew comparing herself to Toni or anyone else was not a good thing to do, but the difference was so stark and it was right here in her face.

Divorced twice—first from a playboy/liar and if that wasn't bad enough, she allowed herself to trust a sweet acting, huggy/kissy rich man who turned out to be a violent narcissist in disguise. There were fading welts and bruises all over her back and legs and breasts that would eventually be gone—but her deeply injured soul would never heal. There was no way to remove the bitterness and disgust at even the memory of the man who treated her as less than a human being. Thankfully, she never had a child—and yet, being childless was the most painful of all her past circumstances. That time for her had passed. Toni and Cowboy were excited about having a late baby, but it was not a planned one. She was sure they wouldn't have planned another child at their ages.

She leaned her back against the front of the stall wall and closed her eyes. What was so different about this place? Toni's home. She almost wanted to feel jealous, but she loved Toni. They were like sisters and she was truly happy for the wonderful life she had here with a man who loved her. She realized then, that's what the difference was. Love. Love lived in this place.

She sat up suddenly when she felt tears drip to her cheeks and swiped them away. At the same moment, a shadow filled the open barn doorway. A tall, lanky cowboy stood staring at her—his horse standing quietly behind him.

"Ms. Julie?"

A smile instantly pulled across her face as she quickly brushed at her cheeks for good measure. "Hello again." She stood up and brushed at the hay pieces on the back of her jeans, still smiling.

AJ removed his hat and smiled back but didn't come inside. The look he was giving her was about to undo her composure. He could see the tear streaks.

"Just having an old memory moment," she explained. "Don't let me be in your way here."

"You're in no one's way, hon. I'm going to bring this tired pony through here and put him up for the day and we sure don't mind the company."

A memory of hanging out on Toni's Uncle John's horse ranch in Texas when they were kids flashed in her mind. "I guess you'll need to brush her and feed her?"

"Him—and that's right. Want to help?"

"I'd love to."

AJ settled his old straw back on his head and led his ranch mount inside, pointing ahead of him down the concrete alleyway. He waited for her to get in step beside him. She didn't miss the gentleman way this cowboy had—removing his hat, waiting for her to walk *beside,* not behind him. These actions didn't mean so much by themselves, but his eyes—his countenance was kind, through and through. She didn't know for sure what she saw in his face—it wasn't familiar to her, but it was drawing her like a magnet.

He stopped in front of the tack room and exchanged the bridle for a halter and unsaddled. He set the saddle on its rack and brought out a curry and soft brush. "Go over him in circular motions with this, then finish with this soft one all over and on his face." He handed her the brushes and after a moment, realized she'd done this before.

"You're not so new at this, are you?"

"Well, yes and no. I did this a lot when Toni and I were kids. Her Uncle John had horses."

"So I've heard. Toni Luke is one of the best hands around here, especially with the young colts. John Barton was the best in his day and he taught her well—although, like John, part of her ability is a God's gift."

She chuckled at that until a glance at his face said he meant it. She didn't really get the God thing. Why would HE be interested in how someone trained horses?

While she finished grooming, he put a scoop of grain and a block of grass hay in the stall, then removed the halter and let the gelding walk on his own into his pen.

"Julie smiled broadly. "Smart horse."

"Yes, he is. He knows where his steak and potatoes are." He chuckled and went to slide and latch the stall door. "I need to put out feed in a few more stalls and fill up water buckets. The rest will be coming in soon."

"I'll help you."

Twenty minutes later they walked out of the barn into the late afternoon sun.

"I appreciate your help, Ms. Julie…and I really enjoyed your company."

"Thank you. I needed this today. It was fun."

"So…how long will you be staying?"

"I meant to be gone already. I only stopped for a quick visit. This is the first time I've seen Toni since her wedding day."

"That's a long time. I saw how excited she was to see you this morning."

She nodded and chewed on her bottom lip. "I'm not sure what I should do. She's having terrible morning sickness. It just started today and it hit her again this afternoon. I hate to leave her like that. I know Judd is working and their daughter is in school all day. Maybe…"

When she didn't finish, he helped her out. "If you don't have anything pressing your time, maybe you could stay another day or so and get in some real visiting with her. I would think twenty years might leave a lot to talk about."

He caught the pained expression that fleetingly crossed her face— her beautiful, slender oval face and almond-shaped eyes. That pain came from his mention of *twenty years to talk about.* Her windblown, straight blonde hair that lay just below her shoulders was beckoning him to touch it and thankfully he turned that desire into a silent chuckle instead. *Get a grip, son. You're a little too old to go there.*

Dismissing the twenty-year flashback that buzzed her brain, she gave him that big, easy smile. "I better go back and check on her." He took her extended hand she offered. "Thank you again, Mr. Call. You truly made my afternoon special."

She left without another word and he watched her walk off toward the house. The *Mr. Call* was definitely telling him his age but making her afternoon special sounded like a hollow dismissal. So, he needed to take her for what she was—a beautiful lady who crossed his path today and woke his heart up a little bit. That was all.

Before heading out to feed the outside pens, he removed his hat, bowed his head and prayed fervently for Julie Langston.

"Hey—I wondered where you went. Your car was still out there, so I knew you were here someplace." Toni had put on a loose, pale yellow shift and fresh makeup—looking like anything except having been sick all day.

"Well, look at you! I thought you'd still be resting." Julie pushed the heavy wooden kitchen door closed and sat at the small table across from Toni. It took her a few seconds to realize she was getting a squinty-eyed half smile aimed at her. "What?" Her eyes widened as she chuckled through a broad smile.

"Don't *what* me, Julie Gayle Langston! I *know* I didn't put that smile on your face or those twinkles in your eyes."

She laughed aloud. "I do not have...all that. I just walked to the barn and...and brushed a horse. Then I chunked out a few blocks of hay."

"Uh-huh. Whose horse did you brush?"

Julie roared with laughter. "You are not my mother."

"No, I'm not, but I'm your best, oldest and dearest friend and this is my ranch and my barn and you're not getting supper tonight until you answer me. So...whose horse did you brush?"

Julie bent over and laughed like she hadn't done in many years. So far this was one stop on her cross-country trip to nowhere that she was glad she'd made. She and Toni seemed to have picked up where they left off twenty years ago and the nicest gentleman she'd ever been around in her life made her want to smile again. Without trying, he'd made her feel like—his equal. Like someone worth talking to.

Finally, she got control. "If you must know, the nice gentleman who I met here this morning came into the barn and I helped him groom and feed. I walked down there to give you time to rest. And I'm cooking supper for your family so ...there." She didn't know where *cooking supper* came from because she hadn't thought it. It just came out her mouth. But that was a great idea.

"AJ Call." Toni grew a little more serious. "*Nice gentleman* is an understatement for that guy. That describes him perfectly. He was in my wedding, too."

"He told me that, but I don't remember him or anyone else other than you, Cowboy and his mother, Maggie. How is she, by the way?"

"Maggie lived in the old ranch house for a couple of years, then met an Italian man who was here on business of some sort. They fell in love, married and then honeymooned back to his home in Positano, Italy. She's been there around seventeen or eighteen years. Loves it!"

"Oh what a lucky lady! I've never been out of this country, but I have heard of Positano—a beautiful coast resort city built on the side of a cliff. I've seen pictures."

"Maybe you should take yourself a vacation there. Maggie says it's warm year-round. You could stay with ..."

The front door opening stopped their conversation.

"Hello...we're in the kitchen," Toni called out.

Judd stepped just inside. "Ladies, I've got a load of starving cowboys hanging all over the back of my truck. Let's go feed 'em before they riot."

Toni jumped up. "Oh, I forgot to tell you. We're eating chuck wagon grub at Highpoint Dude Ranch. Hank's a great cook."

Julie followed them out and hopped in the front seat beside Toni. The back seat was packed with sweaty cowboys fresh off the range. Introductions were informal, at best—hats lifted up and back down on their heads, including more than one wink. She couldn't keep from glancing around at the men in the bed of the truck—disappointed that Mr. Call wasn't there. She wasn't really sure why she felt that, other than wanting to hear more of his kind, respectful way of speaking.

By the time she'd been introduced around in the chow line and encountered Hank, the funny, chuck wagon cook and his spunky wife, Granny Martha, she was feeling like one of the gang. These people had a way of making a spot for you. But—at the same time, a sense of not belonging in a place like this pushed its way in and dampened her spirit. *Who lives like this?* Everybody enjoying each other? So much laughter—men bringing plates of food to their wives and kids—speaking in a similar fashion that AJ Call had spoken to her. Her head was so filled with frightening voice tones and cursing, then screams and pleas from her own mouth. Confusion wanted to swallow her whole—fear that this was only a *be nice we have a guest,* thing.

She quickly straightened her shoulders when she caught Toni's worried expression aimed at her. She would enjoy this visit today, no matter what the truth of it was. She wasn't a kid anymore nor was she the mental captive of an evil demented man. She was free and who knew what some of these laughing, smiling women might be enduring away from the eyes of others.

Following her friend's lead, they sat at a table on the patio by the hot tub and devoured potato salad and roast chicken. "This is the best food I've ever had in my life. What a treat! I mean…a real chuck wagon cookout."

Toni laughed. "We eat out of that wagon for supper every evening…courtesy of Jesse and Donny Brandon. The hands from our ranch and this one work together a lot. Hank Walton and his sweet wife cook a meal every day for both crews. Sometimes different families choose to eat at home. But these cowboys who live in our bunkhouse always eat here."

"So…what is it with everybody around here? I mean…is everyone *always* so jovial—these men so…respectful of their wives? It's like I've sat here and watched a happy picnic scene out of Little House on the Prairie."

Toni laughed aloud. "I've never noticed that. It's just the norm for us here. Don't get me wrong—we've all had our share of family crisis, but as far as the men treating…"

It suddenly dawned on her what Julie meant. She raised her gaze from the plate of food in front of her to her friend's pained expression. "I'm sorry, Jules. I didn't mean…"

"No, don't be sorry. This place…these people are refreshing. It's a nice change…peaceful."

"Maybe a little bittersweet?"

She nodded and lifted her fork for another bite, but the lump that filled her throat made her put it back down.

"Julie, you didn't come here to see me by some last-minute decision to take my exit. And you didn't get that light turned on in those pretty eyes by AJ accidentally either."

"That did not happen and don't be a matchmaker for me. I don't want another man in my life. I've had two too many as it is."

"I promise I'm not doing that. Well…not…I mean…"

"See! You are!"

They both chuckled and began cleaning up their supper area…

"Well," Toni said, "In case you wondered, *he* probably went home after work. He bunks with the other hands part of the time and eats here, otherwise."

Julie frowned at her.

"You know…just in case you were wondering."

They dumped their throwaway dishes and headed for the petting zoo as soon as Julie heard the baby goats.

"So then…where's home for him?"

Toni caught herself before she reacted in jest. Teasing about this stopped right here because of what she had learned of Julie's past relationships. AJ was one of the finest and most respectful gentleman who had ever worked for them—He was loved by all who knew him. His loving influence on Julie, if only for a short time in passing, could make a sweet memory for her to hold on to. And she definitely had room for one of those.

"About twenty miles from here. He has a nice, small, split-level cabin that he built himself about twenty-five years ago—before we knew him."

They entered the goat's pen and Julie's attention went to the tiny solid black kid that ran up to her and dropped down to lay on top of her feet. She bent down and rubbed her hands down it's back, then stroked its face with both hands. The tiny little *baa* sound, strangely made her eyes burn and fill. She scooped it up and wrapped her arms around it like she would a puppy, then buried her face against its neck and cried.

Toni put an arm around her, hugged her and the little furry ball—and prayed silently.

AJ was feeling a little foolish at the path his mind was demanding. He had let too much time pass—too many years enjoying the solitude of the mountain-cabin life he'd worked so hard to carve out for himself.

Cowboying was his life's work. It's what he knew the best, at least.

As a teen, growing up with a single mom had been hard—working a full-time night job as a stocker in a large discount department store to help her buy groceries during his high school years. He'd pick up a Saturday paycheck most weekends doing yard work or subbing for a friend washing dishes in a family owned cafe.

Sunday mornings and evenings were spent in church beside his sweet mom who never forced the issue with him, but chancing breaking her heart for any reason was unacceptable. The kindness and gentleness of that woman was unmatched to this day. He had told her very early on that his dream was to be a cowboy. When that dream remained in him as he got older, she would buy a lariat rope or spurs or the best cowboy hat she could afford—for every gift giving occasion. She kept his closet in new and used boots as his feet grew. Christmas and birthday cards would always end with a *PS—Go be the best cowboy you can be.*

He stretched his legs and propped his sock clad feet on the balcony railing just outside of his loft bedroom. He'd done just *that*—made the best cowboy he could be. He'd made a good living for himself swinging a rope and breaking colts—and lived like he'd done since he was a kid—as a loner. His mom died just after his twenty-fifth birthday and he left his little hometown in Oklahoma for the high country of Wyoming and settled in.

Never tiring of this wild, beautiful land—seeing it, touching it, sometimes tasting it when a bronc was too serious about being the boss, but there was a few times when he tired of the loneliness—yearned for a special woman to share life with. But that *one* never crossed his path. The isolation of his home and working between the

Double OO and High Point didn't leave much room for meeting anyone. Years of time just went on by and here he sat—over fifty years old and—

He slapped his leg and shook his head. What was he doing to himself? It wasn't often he allowed these thoughts to get to him. He knew it was that pretty little visitor of Toni's—Julie with the soft, thick blonde hair, that brought this on. But she'd made it clear she wasn't interested and he didn't care a thing in the world about getting his old heart broke.

Maybe he needed another dog. He missed his sweet Lilly. She had shadowed his every step for nearly fifteen years before he made her stay home and wait for him, fearing his daily trek was too much for her. She lived to be seventeen. He'd buried her several years ago up on the knoll behind his cabin. That's the last time he could remember crying and he guessed he used up a few years' worth of tears over her. He thought they'd never stop. When they finally dried up, he seemed to move through his days by rote, doing whatever was in front of him to do—not feeling one way or the other about anything.

His faith in Jesus never wavered. At least, he didn't think it had. But he did wonder from time to time if God intended his life to be lived without a mate. In fact, he'd out right asked Him if his *rib* was out there somewhere and if she was, could He point the way to her. Course, that was a good year ago—Maybe closer to two.

When Julie's sweet, gorgeous face suddenly formed in the front of his mind, he shook his head and smiled—got up and headed to bed. He had scattered calves to gather come morning.

But—hours later, he was staring at the ceiling, then out the sliding balcony glass doors, before ending with his face toward a wall with a collage of old pictures of him and a few of his mom that he'd put together decades ago. The framed mixture of his only tangible childhood memories was highly prized—especially the picture of his mom which he'd placed in the center of the frame—the one time he'd taken her out for dinner and a movie just because she worked so hard. Her favorite was barbecue beef ribs and she had smeared the sauce across her mouth, then laughed and smiled big for his pocket camera.

Anne Call. She'd never married but gave birth to AJ in an old motel room with only a young Spanish girl who worked there to help her. Her parents, his grandparents, had banished her from their home and lives when she told them she was pregnant. She never saw them again.

From his earliest memories of her, she spoke to him daily about Jesus and he'd accompanied her to church all his life. It was just the two of them. She lived to raise him and while still a beautiful young woman—she left suddenly during her sleep one night to go be with Jesus. His grief was unfathomably deep for the next few weeks until she had come to visit him in a dream to tell him to go live his life— She was happy.

Within a month, he quit his ranch job in Oklahoma, packed his truck and drove until he reached Jackson Hole, Wyoming.

The next thing he knew, day was breaking outside the sliding doors showing a hazy streak of orange down low through the pines. By the time he was dressed for work, he had just enough time to get a bite of breakfast at High Point before saddling up at the Double OO. He felt well rested and starved. His first hour of the day usually consisted of cold water in the face, coffee and prayer. Maybe it was the sweet smell of fall in the air this morning or going to sleep last night with memories of his mother. This just felt like it was going to be a good day.

And yes! He was going to get a new pup. It was time.

AJ picked up a paper plate and handed it to the cook. "Fill it up, Hank. I'm running on empty this morning."

"I can fix you right up, cowboy."

It took two hands to hold the flimsy plate after Hank doubled up on eggs, bacon, sausage, fried potatoes and biscuits and gravy. A smoking styrofoam cup of black coffee was grasped in his palm while the plate balanced on the top of his wrist. When he felt the plate shift, he stopped just before reaching a table, unsure of his next move. Before deciding if he could continue, two hands lifted the plate away.

"That was close. Good thing I was watching you walk over here."

He looked up to see the smiling face of the one who'd kept him awake for hours the past night. "Good morning and thank you. You saved my day before it even started. I'm eternally grateful, mam." He grinned at her and followed her with his coffee to a table where the Luke's were seated.

"I just rescued this handsome cowboy's breakfast so he's at my mercy today." Julie laughed and set his plate beside hers.

"Hey there, AJ." Judd rose up and reached across the table to shake hands. "Sounds like you just got yourself into a whole mess of trouble." He tilted his head toward Julie, who was still smiling from ear to ear.

"Hi, AJ." Toni wasn't her usual jovial self. Either she just sat down or wasn't hungry. Her plate was still full.

"Hi, AJ." Jenny licked at the butter on her biscuit, then wiped her mouth. "Dad, I'll get on the bus from here with Anna Leigh. They're leaving—I gotta go. Bye everybody."

"Hello, Jenny. Bye, Jenny," AJ waved and chuckled.

"Honey?" Toni's face had paled and she wasn't sure her legs would hold her up.

Judd jumped up and rushed to the opposite side of the picnic table to help her. "Is it morning sickness or something more?"

"I'm sick. Help me get to the truck."

Julie jumped up and Toni waved her away. "Stay here and enjoy your morning. I'll be okay in a little while."

When others noticed the commotion, some headed their way, but Judd waved them off. "Morning sickness. I'm taking her home."

Julie and AJ settled back on the bench and started eating.

He began shaking his head. "Man alive—these mamas go through a lot getting their babies into this world."

"I've never been through it, but I've seen and heard stories. I think it would be worth it for just nine months of discomfort."

"Good way to look at it and I agree. Course, that agreement might not count for a hill of beans coming from the *man* of the nine months."

She laughed aloud. "Oh, I think it would with all the pampering and holding her head over the potty while she puked and doing lots of back rubs."

He shoved in a bite of biscuit and gravy, chewed fast and swallowed before he laughed it out all over the table. "It's a good thing I'm a well-seasoned cow poop kicker with that kind of talk over my eggs."

She slapped a hand over her mouth and giggled. "I'm sorry."

"Oh, not a problem. You should see what happens to my peanut butter sandwich hanging on the side of my saddle after it's chased and roped a few calves. I quit bothering to look at it. I just eat it."

Julie put a hand over her face, lost in a fit of giggles. When he glanced at her, the laughter rubbed off and he laughed like he hadn't done in a long time.

"Mercy. Where have you been all my life?" She swiped tears off both her cheeks.

He watched her pull herself together. He'd never once wanted to reach out this bad and touch a woman's hair, her face or close his fingers around her slender waist. "I've been right here for probably most of it—waiting for you to get here."

Both of them sat like mannequins, staring at each other. No one was laughing, but two hearts were pounding in unison. He wanted to back up a sentence or two, but he'd already put it out there. He waited for her to cut and run and he wouldn't blame her—too much, too fast.

Finally, "I don't know what to say to that." She'd been drawn to him from the moment she saw him standing in Toni's doorway. She almost felt like a tongue-tied schoolgirl.

"Well…I would like to tell you that I said that without thinking first. And it would be partly true. But I really have enjoyed our little bit of time together—at the barn yesterday and here this morning. So…I'm hoping you'll tell me that you'll be staying here for a while longer."

"Okay."

"Okay?"

She smiled. "I actually agreed with Judd last night to stay for a while and look out for Toni while he's working, until she gets over being so sick. I would enjoy spending some time with you."

"I'm glad to hear that. And right this minute, I better head to work. Can I give you a ride back to Toni's?"

"Thank you."

They cleaned their table off and made small talk on the way to the ranch. He stopped close to the back of the house. After stepping out, she turned around and looked him in his eyes. "AJ, thank you for being a kind man." She closed the door and went inside.

***

CHAPTER SEVEN

AJ let his cow pony trot off his cool morning friskies before heading down to search out the brush and brambles for hidden or lost calves. Most of the snow had melted.

He was trying to savor every minute of this day—Something had changed, it seemed, overnight. The atmosphere, the air around him felt different. Even *he* felt a weightlessness of his own body with every move his horse made—like he couldn't feel the saddle beneath him or the usual ache or muscle pain from day after day in a saddle. He wasn't sure what was happening, but he did know it was a supernatural something and he fully intended to enjoy it for however long it lasted.

Time could prove him wrong, but deep inside he felt that he knew that he knew that that little green-eyed lady he'd just dropped off at the Luke's home was connected to him in a big way. He couldn't' stop himself from envisioning her walking hand in hand with him for the rest of his life. He could see her in his kitchen—in his bed—enjoying ranch life together with that sweet sound of laughter filling his house.

He wondered what her special pass-time was—her hobbies? What did she enjoy doing the most? Dislike the most? He wanted to know everything about her. What happened to her during the past twenty years?

He reined his horse into a walk when he saw some of the hands within shouting distance. He needed a minute to calm down—get his mind on the business at hand, if that was even possible and act like a fifty-two-year-old man instead of a schoolboy.

He shifted his weight in his stirrup, hard to one side, to center the saddle on his gelding's back. *A kind man,* she'd called him. And she didn't have that big pretty smile on her face when she said it. She was serious.

Toni was able to make it a couple of hours between bouts of nausea and weakness. The smell of food cooking or coffee brewing seemed to trigger another round. She didn't have morning sickness to speak of with either of her first two children. She hardly knew what to do with this, but the doctor said everything was normal—this happened sometimes.

Julie passed the hours while Toni lay in bed, by dusting and cleaning floors. She loved to cook and bake but was afraid the smells would make it worse for the morning sickness. She did make a pot of homemade vegetable soup and insisted Toni try to hold some of it down. She needed some kind of nourishment for her and the baby both.

"Jules, this is *sooo* good. You were a good cook when we were in high school. If I puke it up, don't get offended, because I'm really enjoying it at the moment."

"Go slow—Sip on the broth."

"Thank you for staying with me, Julie. I know Judd really appreciates it." She spooned a few sips of broth, savoring the perfection of the mild seasonings. "So, what's on your *other* agenda today?"

Julie stared at her, a slight smirk pulling her lips.

"You know, besides babysitting me."

"Not a thing…yet…that I know of."

"So, he's supposed to call you, then?"

She couldn't stop the smile on her face or the twinkle that darted into her eyes. "Yes."

"Wonderful! And when he does, you go and enjoy yourself. He's a sweetheart of a man. *Do not* rush back here because of me. I can puke and sleep without your assistance."

She chuckled, wondering how her life could go from dark to light without a plan to make it happen. Life just seemed to have shifted gears when she wasn't looking.

"We've just become friends—nothing more. We enjoyed talking this morning at breakfast and he had to rush off to work. We decided to pick up later where we had to stop. That's all."

"Okay…I'm…glad and…going to be sick. Trash can! Trash can!"

Julie wheeled and grabbed the tall kitchen garbage can, sliding it under Toni's face just in time. She pulled a clean dish towel out of the cabinet drawer behind her, wet it with cold water and put it in Toni's outstretched hand. She pulled out the chair beside her and sat down, gently patting her back and wishing she could do something to help.

"I need to lay down. I'm sorry, Jules."

"Oh no, you don't be sorry. Come on, I'll help you to your bed." With an arm around her trembling shoulders, she held on to her as she walked on wobbly legs to the opposite end of the house.

When she pushed open the heavy wooden double doors to the master bedroom, three-steps down entered the beautifully decorated sunken bed and bath that was pure romance. She couldn't remember ever seeing this room before, but it was, by far, the most elegantly cozy place in the home. The ceramic tiled floor was beige with brick red streaks shooting through the large squares. Several white woven rugs were placed on either side and at the foot of the huge king log bed. Turquoise and deep red and tan covered the bed in a quilted comforter and large pillows. Her eye traveled to the aged-distressed turquoise window shutters. The decor was flawless, yet so warm and peaceful feeling.

Toni curled up on her far side of the bed, moaning with nausea misery and Julie pulled covers up around her.

Stepping through the double doors into the bathroom had to be similar to walking out into an island paradise complete with a rocked-in pool and waterfall—vines and flowering greenery growing in crevices in the rocks around the pool and up the back of the wall. The floor was a mock through-the-woods pathway bordered with flowers and greenery. Not in her wildest dreams could she have ever come up with a master suite such as this. Who does this kind of thing?—Maybe young lovers who plan on keeping their love strong and alive.

She grabbed a washcloth, wet it and hurried back and handed it to Toni. She laid it over her face, then waved Julie away.

After cleaning up in the kitchen, she found the shaded back patio and stretched out in a fancy lounge chair. She closed her eyes for a moment to savor the memories she'd made early that morning with AJ, then nearly left her chair in one fluid move when a hand closed over her shoulder.

"Whoa...don't have a runaway. It's me Judd."

"Oh gosh, I was dreaming something, but you scared it off." She glanced around and realized she'd been asleep for a while. The sun was almost down.

"I don't know how long you've been out here, but I believe you're fully cooked to the bone."

She stood up and pushed her hair from her face. When her fingernails slightly raked across her forehead, she got what Judd just said. "Ouch. I thought it was shady here."

"It is until the sun drops just above those trees there, then you get rays for a couple hours."

She touched her neck and chest where the V-neck T-shirt she wore exposed her skin. It was tender. She was just thankful she had on jeans and long sleeves.

"We're about to leave for High Point to eat supper. You've got about five minutes."

"Oh mercy, I think I'll stay here. This sunburn needs my attention more than my stomach does. Is Toni alright?"

"She just woke up and is okay for now. Can we bring you back a plate?"

"No, thank you. I made soup today. I'll have that if I get hungry."

A dually pulled through the circle drive to where they were standing. She recognized AJ's truck and watched as he got out and came toward them.

"Hey, AJ. Just about to take the crew to get a bite to eat."

He nodded in affirmation, "I saw you standing here and thought I'd offer this young lady a ride over if she wants to continue our visit from this morning."

Judd looked from one to the other and nodded his head. "Good deal. I'll get my crew and head that way then." He went inside to round up his beautiful, pregnant bride.

AJ smiled and tipped his bare head. "Evening, Ms. Julie." He held his hat in one hand that hung down at his side. The other hand was relaxed with his thumb resting in his front jeans pocket.

"Hi. I'm sorry…I'm not really hungry and I got a sunburn I need to do something for." She still felt a little rum-drum with sleep.

"I see that. Do you have anything to put on those burns?"

She thought a second. "Moisturizing cream. That'll have to do for now. I stupidly fell asleep out here."

"That sounds like something I would do. It's easy to relax and enjoy the outdoors around here."

She ran her fingers through her hair and pushed it back from her face, lightly scraping her forehead again. "Ow. That's really burned."

"Yes, mam, it is. I have a healing oil that was given to me when I got a bad burn a few months back. It works fast, but it's at my house. I could run up and get it for you."

"But, that's twenty miles from here. I'm sure it will be better by tomorrow.

His eyes widened slightly, realizing he'd been the topic of discussion—probably with Toni. How else would she know how far away he lived? "Well…I have an idea, if you feel comfortable with it. Would you like to ride out to my place with me to get the oil? It's a nice drive and…"

"Yes, I would."

He grinned, feeling a schoolboy euphoria at her quick acceptance.

"Give me a couple minutes. I'll be right back." She went inside to grab her purse and almost changed her mind after glancing in the foyer mirror. Her face and neck were beet red! But she *needed* that oil and she *wanted* to spend the evening with AJ..

Less than an hour later, AJ turned to cross a cattleguard and headed up through an open pasture toward a tree line about a quarter of a mile out. Once they entered the trees and headed upward, the gorgeous tall Ponderosa pines seemed to swallow the dually whole—the shaded beauty that enveloped them made her suck in a breath of sheer awe.

"This might look a little scary since it's a strange place to you. It got dark on us, but it's not that far through here to the house."

She loved the way he made sure she was comfortable being with him on this trip... They were, after all, virtual strangers. But she felt completely safe because of Toni and Judd's long-time relationship with him—It was easy to allow herself to really like and enjoy his company.

He turned on his bright headlights now as darkness covered them and blotted out the trees, except where the truck lights shined on them. The path through the trees wasn't more than a jeep road. It was only a few yards until they drove up on a mountain styled cabin—a rustic log with a front porch that set on the ground and was fully covered by a roof held up with huge long poles. The headlights were the only light, but Julie felt anything but afraid. A crazy excitement rushed through her middle.

Stopping in front of the porch, he glanced at her face. The pleased wide eyes he saw made him smile—glad that he had brought her here. "Ms. Julie, I can run in and get the oil or you're welcome to come in."

Even though she had begun to feel more effects of the sunburn—tight, hot skin and slightly nauseated, she wasn't going to let that ruin her evening. "I would love to see your house. I bet this is beautiful to see in the daylight."

"Well, I'm kind of fond of this place. It's been home for a lot of years. I'll open up and turn on some lights." He got out and jogged to the front door, keys in his hand.

In seconds, lights lit up the porch and the interior that she could see through the windows. She reached to turn off the truck headlights and got out.

He held the door open for her to go inside and she was amazed at the openness of the unique interior. From the front door, she could view the kitchen, dining and den areas without moving a step. Although the house had no dividing walls, each area was set up in such a way that the rooms were obviously individual from each other. The furnishings were sparse, but a warm mixture of perfect country mountain cabin. At least, that would be her description of it, along with just *sweet.* Home decorating and design had always been of great interest to her. She couldn't help but take in the details.

When she turned to look back at him, he was eyeing her strangely and for a few seconds, the room began to spin.

"I think I'll sit down for a…"

Her legs wobbled and he stepped to her, wrapping an arm around her shoulders when she looked like she might pass out.

"I'm…fine," she muttered and tried to grasp the back of a chair close by.

"I can see that." He easily scooped her up in one motion and carried her to a tightly stuffed, blue plaid lounge chair where she could comfortably recline. "Julie, are you sick at your stomach with this? Tell me what you're feeling."

"No, but my head hurts and I'm freezing. I'm so sorry."

"Lay still. I'll be right back."

She watched him race up a short staircase, then heard a cabinet door open and shut and water running. He came down and handed her a small, wet towel.

"Put this on your neck and face to cool down that burn. Can you take Ibuprofen?"

"I take it at night sometimes. It helps me sleep."

He went into the kitchen and returned with a large glass of tap water and two capsules. By that time, she was shaking with feverish chills. He retrieved a patchwork quilt that was folded and laying on one end of a small bench in the dining room. After spreading it over her, he dragged an old ladder-back chair up beside her and took her pulse.

"I'm giving you about thirty or forty minutes to be a little better or we're heading into the hospital emergency. Drink all that water you can."

"Are you a doctor or nurse?"

"Not even close, but I had a little paramedic training a couple years ago. The hospital in Jackson offered evening classes and I thought it might be a good thing to have. Fact is, you're my first patient. Aren't you the lucky one?"

His grin made her want to reach up and touch his cheek. The sweet, caring qualities this man had, not to mention his handsome face and sexy cowboy physique, would melt the heart of any woman, including the young ones. She couldn't help wondering about his back-story in the female department. He *had* to have one. "So, do you have a diagnosis yet?"

"As a matter of fact, mam, I do. I'm fairly sure you have a mild case of sun poisoning."

Her eyebrows drew together, not sure if he meant that as a joke. "Is that a real thing?"

"It is. Let's give you a few minutes for the meds to work. Also…" he handed her a small bottle, "gently rub a little of this Eucalyptus oil on your face and chest. It's good stuff."

She applied it and lay her head back, pulling the quilt up around her neck. After laying the cool towel back around her neck, she closed her eyes and willed her body to stop shaking.

He relaxed deeper into the straight-backed chair and watched her shivering beneath the quilt. She was so physically beautiful; it was hard to not touch her cheek or her hair—or to lean down and kiss her softly on the mouth. He dated a few women over his years, but none had ever had this effect on him. How was he supposed to respond to this? He had no idea if she felt a thing in the world for him personally and probably didn't. They were strangers. She didn't know what he was like—except that he'd been *kind* to her and that seemed to impact her most. But every man on the ranch, both ranches, would treat her respectfully. It made him wonder though, that she had specifically thanked him for being kind to her. And he wondered even more how he was going to feel when she was no longer here in his cabin for him to take care of when she needed someone?

He knew he was thinking like a demented love-starved old cowboy that needed to shake himself back to reality. *Wow, Lord, could You help a man out here? I can't make this lady fall in love with me and I need to throw on the brakes of this old heart—but* —He looked at her now sleeping soundly—*I don't know how.*

He checked her pulse again. It was slower—more normal and her slender fingers and wrist were cool. The chills had backed off as well and he pulled the quilt to one side of her. When she didn't move a muscle, he got up and quietly went out the front door, moving without sound to keep from waking his house guest.

The tree limbs were swaying in a wind that was stronger than normal—the air was Fall-crispy and he lowered himself silently into his homemade porch swing to savor his favorite kind of evening.

He didn't care if Julie slept all night—but from the sound of the wind picking up by the second, he realized something was brewing. He hadn't listened to a weather report or heard talk of it at the ranch, so this caught him off guard.

He got up and went around the side of the house where he could see that his two mares had made their way into the small barn. He had a ten-acre pasture that they ran on with a one-hundred-gallon galvanized water tub just inside the fence.

He hurried out to close the barn gate and tossed a half bale of grass hay into their inside feeder. Glancing over the top of the gate, he saw that the barn water trough was still full.

"Goodnight, ladies," he threw out to the mares and reached the front porch just as the rain hit. The wind was howling now, slamming water onto the porch. Once inside, he closed the heavy wooden door as gently as possible and bolted it.

Julie was still sleeping soundly. After checking her again, he wondered at the pain meds he'd given her. She told him they helped her sleep and he was realizing now that she was probably ultra-sensitive to that kind of medication.

He went upstairs to the desk in the corner of his loft bedroom to see if he could get a call out to the Double OO. Toni answered and he let her know the situation of her house guest, but the line went dead before he finished the conversation. At least they knew where she would be tonight.

After thinking about her possibly sleeping all night in that chair—he immediately stripped the bed sheets off his bed and put his only other set on. He made it up as smooth and comfortable as possible with fresh quilts and pillowcases, locked the balcony doors and headed back downstairs.

He was hungry and figured she would be waking up that way soon. A large can of beef stew should work, he decided, after searching his pantry and fridge. He had orange juice, which would be good for her and coffee. He never had company out here, so didn't plan that way when he grocery shopped.

After he ate a bowl of stew and handful of saltines, he went back up the steps to the first landing where the bathroom was located and did a quick clean up. It wasn't in too bad of shape—he was rarely home to use it much.

Remembering suddenly that she had brought a purse with her, he went back out, slicker over his head and grabbed it from the front floor of the dually and put it on the lamp table beside her chair.

The storm hadn't let up but seemed to be more intense with thunder and lightning. The wind came in gusts that whipped the boughs of the pines without mercy.

Standing just inside the front door, he prayed—*Lord, let Your angels surround all the folks at High Point and the Double OO—their animals and homes and thank You for taking care of all that concerns me and Ms. Julie. In Jesus Name, Amen.*

When he got back inside, he decided to try and wake her so she could eat and then go back to bed upstairs where she'd be comfortable. He took her hand and squeezed slightly until she began

98

to stir. She tried to open her eyes but couldn't fully get there. She smiled at him, then let her eyes close.

"Ms. Julie, can you wake up? I need to know you're all right."

"Okay."

"Did the pain medicine make you sleep this way?"

"Yesh."

He knew that was possible in some people. "I made you a comfortable bed. Let's see if we can get you in it."

"Okay."

After he got her to stand on her feet, he grasped her upper arms from behind and guided her up to the loft.

She poured herself onto the bed like a drunk might do. He couldn't help but be amused, but he knew this girl had no business taking those particular meds again. He removed her white tennis shoes and checked her pulse again before covering her with the quilt and turning off the big overhead light.

After cleaning up in the kitchen and shutting off the lights, he pulled out a couple quilts and extra pillow from the storage closet just outside the bathroom, deciding to sleep in his recliner next to the bed. He knew she'd used this over-the-counter medication as a sleep aid before—not a good idea—but, he felt the need to stay close until it wore off a little.

With the lamp light turned off, the room was pitch dark except for a streak of lightening ever so often. He could see her body curled up beneath the blankets and he thought it odd at how natural it felt with this woman in his house—his bed. He listened to her steady breathing.

The sight of her lumpy form in his bed stirred something in him far deeper than just lust because she was a beautiful female in his private space. It was far more than that. He'd never in all his adult life felt this—almost like this woman was part of him—his life, his body—He didn't really know how to define what he felt.

Her blonde hair was splayed across his pillow in a jumbled mess of gorgeous. It crossed his mind what Judd Luke had preached on one Sunday a long time back, but he never forgot it—at least, not the main idea of the sermon. It was something about God creating Eve for

Adam out of one of his own ribs—And in similar fashion, He had created a certain woman for a man today. If he waited until she crossed his path in life, they would know that they were meant to be together—their love would be only for each other.

He had given up on that notion, though. He was in his fifties now and on the downhill slide of his life. He'd let go of such a thing happening for him—until now. Until Julie Langston. Did she carry his rib, so to speak? *Lord?*

He closed his eyes and fell asleep almost immediately.

When he opened his eyes again, the sun was peeking through the pines out of the balcony glass doors—and a pair of smiling, green eyes were bearing down on him from his bed, the owner propped on an elbow.

"Good morning, kind sir."

He smiled and set up, pushing the foot of the recliner down and raking his hand through his hair at the same time. "Good morning, sleeping beauty. I thought I might have to raise you from the dead last night."

She sat up then and swung her legs over the edge of the bed, almost bumping her knee against his. She fixed her eyes on his for several seconds and shook her head. "I can't believe you gave me your bed and slept in that chair. I honestly expected you to crawl in beside me."

He studied her a long moment. "I can't believe you remember last night."

"I was extremely sleepy—not unconscious. I got up and found the bathroom a couple hours ago. You were sleeping so sound, I decided not to wake you up."

Does that medicine I gave you always knock you out like that?"

"Pretty much, except I only take one."

He shook his head then and glanced away for a second. "I wish you'd have said something."

"I'm sorry about that. I felt so sick, I really didn't think about it. I just…wish you had shared this big old bed with me."

He leaned forward and gazed into her face with all seriousness. "Julie, if the day ever comes that I share a bed with you, you'll be fully awake and aware and in agreement—even if it's just to lay there fully clothed and sleep. I abhor disrespect in a man toward a woman—in any situation. And crawling in bed with you last night, in your condition..."

They stared at each other a few seconds.

"If I had asked you to lay beside me...and hold me...would you have done that for me?"

He held her gaze, his heart racing, and slowly nodded his head up and down. "Yes, mam, I would have."

"Would you...hold me now?"

Without hesitating a split second, he reached and took her hand and pulled her onto his lap. He leaned the recliner back and wrapped both of his arms tightly around her as she curled up as close as she could get and buried her face against his chest.

They were quiet for a while—she savored the close, secure embrace of two strong arms branding her with a sense of being loved that she'd craved her whole life and never found—He, so gently, moved her thick strands of hair away from covering her eyes, even though he couldn't see them. He caressed her hair feeling the soft texture in his thin, leathery fingers. She felt like a small child curled in his lap, but his emotions were exploding for the woman that she was.

AJ closed his eyes, continuing to thread his fingers in her tangled hair while keeping her hostage in his arms. When he couldn't stand it any longer, he loosened his grip and shifted in the chair, causing her to lift her head and her face to his. He ran his fingers into the side of her hair, letting his gaze run sensually at her hair, her eyes, her lips. This woman was his—And he was hers. He knew it. When he lowered his head to touch his lips to hers, a feather-light touch—she reached up and splayed her hand on his cheek and leaned up to ask for more. They kissed with more passion than either of them had ever known about.

They finally came apart out of necessity—for oxygen. Breathing hard and fast, they both began to laugh.

"We *are* good kissers, aren't we?" She wiped a smear of wetness off the top of his upper lip, still giggling.

"Woman, this could kill a man my age who doesn't have the sense to come up for air." His grin showed his beautiful, straight, white teeth.

She became quiet, staring into his eyes. "You seem like a dream I'm having that I'm fighting to not wake up from." She watched his smiling face take on a look of disbelief. "I sound ridiculous, I know. I just..." She hesitated a long while.

"Just what, pretty lady."

"Just that...I don't want you to move your arms from around me...to stop holding me so tight or...to stop kissing me like you just did."

He said nothing for a minute but held her with that incredulous stare.

"I know I sound like I'm reading from a sappy old love story and I'm..."

"Julie," he interrupted, "what I would really...*really* love to do right now is take every thread you're wearing off of you, put you in my bed and make love to you until neither one of us can take anymore. But..."

"I knew there was going to be a *but*." She tried to get up from his lap, but he held her in place.

"Wait a minute now. All *buts* are not bad. *But*—I want us to slow down just a little. Spend lots of time together and get to know each other. You don't know anything about me...or me, you."

She closed her eyes and swallowed hard, before cutting her gaze back to his face. "You do realize that I'm not planning to be here long, don't you?"

"Yes, I know that. I'm hoping you will decide to stay." He paused and smiled. "I *really* want you to."

Her arms went around his neck and she kissed him softly on the lips. "For now, I will. I need to help Toni while she's having morning sickness. And—we'll see how we feel about each other after that. And—for now, I better call her and let her know where I am."

"They know you stayed with me last night. I called."

"Okay, well...I'm starved. I guess we can start by finding out what we like to eat." She got up and stretched. "Then I better go see how Toni is doing."

He stood and pulled her against him and kissed her warmly, holding her elbow. "I meant what I said. I really want to spend time with you. A *lot* of time."

"Me, too," she whispered.

"By the way, your sunburn looks seventy-five percent better."

She touched her cheeks, then forehead. "It's not very sore now. And, by the way, I haven't thanked you for taking care of me last night."

"You're welcome. It was my pleasure. I say we go grab a bite at the chuck wagon, then I'll drop you off at the Luke's. How does that sound?"

"Perfect." She went down the steps into the bathroom remembering that she'd seen her purse, containing her makeup and hairbrush, in there earlier. She smiled as she closed the door behind her. Never in her wildest imagination could she have dreamed up a man like this one. She had no idea such a gorgeous, muscled-up cowboy gentleman even existed outside of a romance novel—but there was and she found him—or he found her. Either way, she already hated the thought of being away from his side for one day. He was right though—They should slow down. She just hoped she could keep from making a fool of herself through this slow-down—She already felt hopelessly in love with the man.

***

CHAPTER EIGHT

Daisy stepped out on the back porch of the cabin and thought someone had surely left a door open in Heaven—The past night's storm had ended, but the wind was blowing a crisp Fall invigorating north breeze that felt so peaceful. So far, she had found nothing about this new place and lifestyle that wasn't a pure pleasure to experience.

Maybe that was because the most important part of her life was in place—her cowboy-to-the-bone husband was in love with her, even at her very worst. His devotion to her was one hundred percent opposite from anyone who'd been in her life as far back as she could remember. He was handsome, strong and gentle, putting her needs—even her *wants* ahead of himself. He observed what she liked to eat, drink and little things she would mention that she wanted to experience some day.

Mitch had been inadvertently teaching her how to love. She'd lived without love in every aspect of her life and hadn't recognized her deficiency in being able to show the love she felt inside for anyone—including her husband who she adored and loved with her whole heart and soul.

For more than a year, she had been on the receiving end of Mitch's promise to love and care for her night and day—to hold her tight through every nightmare and hurtful memory that she would have. And he never failed her even once.

Today, she had a strong desire to do something for him—something a little more than the ordinary. But, what?

She had the oddest desire to go visit Laura Brandon. She had felt that for the past couple of days. Maybe she could give her some ideas of how she could show Mitch how much she loved him.

Mama dog was gaining weight and had become attached to her like a small child to its mother. She took excellent care of her two babies and when they slept, she followed Daisy's every move through the cabin, jumping into her lap when she sat down. The little dog was her happiest when Daisy gave her a treat of a little warm milk with her food and a minute or two of her arms squeezing her tight, especially just before turning out the cabin lights at bedtime.

Old Samson seemed in agreement with the smaller dog's attachment to his long-time person. He continued a vigilant watch over the three newcomers, especially at night, but napping off and on in a corner of the back porch during the day.

Mitch had left out before daybreak for the Double OO and probably wouldn't be back before supper time. So—maybe she'd drive up to the ranch yard and try to visit with Laura. She'd had a close connection with her on her first vacation trip here, sort of the motherly type who she could trust and confide in.

The sun was up and bright when she parked her car in the drive beside the Brandon's home. Breakfast had ended about an hour or more before and everyone had gone on about their day.

Just as she stepped out of her vehicle, Laura pushed the kitchen door open and waved her inside.

"Daisy, what a nice surprise. Come inside and have some coffee."

"Thank you. I was hoping you were home."

They exchanged a hug and Daisy scrubbed her shoes on the scratchy brown mat at the door before stepping inside.

Laura immediately pulled two cups from the cabinet above the coffee pot and poured from the fresh pot she'd just dripped. "I must have known a coffee drinking friend was going to surprise me this morning. Just cream, right?"

"Yes. You have a good memory."

"Oh…I remember things about special friends I make. Would you like to sit in the den? The patio is still a little wet from the storm."

Daisy sat on one end of the small sofa and Laura sat beside her on the other end, with one leg curled beneath her so she was turned halfway toward her guest.

"I haven't seen you and Mitch here for chow time in a while. I hope everything's going good."

She nodded. "Yes, mam, everything is wonderful. I have so much time on my hands that I've been cooking our meals. It gives me something to do."

"That's good, Daisy. I don't know of a man on the earth who wouldn't love home cooking every day."

"I know Mitch appreciates it. That's sort of what…I wanted to ask you about."

"Cooking?"

"No…yes…well, I know I keep things clean in the cabin and outside, too and cook for him, but…"

Laura sat quietly and waited for her to form what she wanted to say.

"He loves me so much, Laura. And he shows it in every way possible. I love him just as much…but, I don't know how to *show* him. I *feel* it so intense at times that I could nearly burst, but I don't know what special things I can do to *show* it."

"Hello! Is this private or can I come in?"

"In here, Martha. Grab you some coffee. I just made it. Daisy, we can continue this later if you want, but Granny Martha is good with private conversation."

"No, she's welcome. Maybe both of you together can give me some ideas."

"Ideas for what?" Granny came in and looked from one to the other while slurping a sip of hot liquid. "If you two are planning some kind of shenanigan, I'm in!" She plopped down in Laura's big easy chair as the two women burst out laughing.

"Daisy is looking for a fresh idea to surprise Mitch—to make him feel special."

Daisy lowered her gaze to the floor, realizing Laura hadn't understood. Something was missing inside of her. She didn't know what it was—an emptiness inside of her. She wasn't sure she could explain what she was feeling.

Laura and Granny Martha suddenly exchanged glances as they realized there was something more to this.

"Honey, what's bothering you? We're having some silly fun, but I believe there's something you're not saying."

"I don't know how to say it." She paused to think. "I get so much love and attention from Mitch. I know how much *he* loves *me,* but I don't believe he knows *my* love for *him.*" She chuckled nervously. "Does that make any sense at all?"

Laura bobbed her head up and down while Martha copied her movement. "Daisy, your fear of not being enough for your husband is not unusual. Most of us wives that you know on this ranch have probably felt the same way at some point, but especially early in our marriages."

"That's the truth, Daisy," Granny scooted to the edge of her chair and set her coffee mug on the lamp table. "Here's the way it works— These cowboys are some of the hardest working men you'll ever meet. They love what they do and sunup to sundown is the law of ranching. Everyone of em' on this ranch has good, hard working women to come home to—and all our men treat us like we're his queen."

Laura and Daisy were both fixed on her face, taking in every word.

"And they do that because *they* don't feel like they quite measure up to their wife. I'd bet you keep your Mitch in clean house and clean clothes and good food bought and cooked up and ready for him when he drags in at night, don't you?"

"Yes, mam, I do all that."

"So, what is it that makes you feel loved the most that he does for you?"

She thought about it a minute, even though she didn't need to. That answer came to her mind instantly. "When he holds me in his arms because I…have nightmares sometimes," she shot a glance at Laura, then back to Granny, "and he just holds me to let me know I'm safe. The way he looks at me most of the time, loving me through his eyes."

Granny scooted back in the chair. "Well, sister, there's your answer."

"What do you mean?"

Laura understood and swallowed hard to stop her emotions from surfacing. She had just realized where she was probably not measuring up so well for her own husband. Jesse was exactly how Daisy had just described Mitch and she knew she needed to give back a little better for him.

"Daisy, Martha means that both you and Mitch work hard for each other in every way you possibly can, but in the intimate times, in the same way that he makes you feel the most loved—simply do the same for him. Give him the security of your arms around him. Hold him tight—let him see the love light shining from *your* eyes. You be *his* soft place to fall."

Laura could see in her widening eyes that she got it. And so did she! She hadn't given nearly as much as she'd gotten in that area from her Jesse.

"Me and Hank are side by side most days." Martha waved her hand toward the outside wall, "doing the fixins for the chuck wagon and he helps me sometimes with laundry and cleaning the cabins. But we make the most of our private times when we hug and hold each other and look, really look, in each other's eyes. He goes away from that knowing how I feel and I know his feelings for me. Oh…and don't forget to laugh."

"What am I supposed to laugh at?" Daisy just wanted her to keep talking.

"Every one of his jokes. Even if they're the dumbest thing you ever heard. Hank laughs at me all the time. He thinks I'm plumb funny, so I just bust out cackling at his jokes, even if they don't make sense half the time."

Granny started giggling when she saw Daisy and Laura were both laughing behind their hands. She stood up and picked up her coffee mug. "You ladies enjoy your day now. Me and Hank are headed to town for groceries."

Daisy got up and collected both empty cups to deposit in the kitchen sink. "She should go into the counseling business—hang a shingle out on the chuck wagon."

Laura laughed. "Maybe we should make her one and let her find it hanging on the wagon. That lady is full of wisdom—such good advice."

"Yes! Let's do it. I've got painting supplies at home." Daisy clapped her hands with a prankster gleam in her eye.

"You're on, girlfriend."

They high-fived and Daisy left, realizing as she drove home that the empty spot inside of her was filled up—with hope and know-how and joy. More than ever, she wanted to be a part of the other people's lives that lived here—to get to know them and share conversation and a cup of coffee. It seemed as if an unfamiliar yet welcomed beam of light had broken through the wall of her damaged soul.

AJ could see loose strands of blonde hair blowing in the breeze before he ever reached the Lukes log ranch house. Julie was crouched and bent over the flower beds that circled around one side of the back patio.

The sound of an approaching dually brought her slowly up on her feet, one hand shading the sun from her eyes. Her heart couldn't help itself—it picked up a faster rhythm, causing her to involuntarily splay a hand over her chest.

A broad smile greeted him as he sauntered up in all his work dust and cow smells. "Hey girl." He pulled his hat off and returned her smile.

"Hey yourself."

"I was looking for a supper date. I've got reservations for two...for Italian in Jackson Hole. Interested?"

"So...if I can't go, who's your next choice?"

"You."

"Then, who's your last choice?"

"You."

"I need a bath."

"Me, too. I'll clean up and pick you up in…what?"

"An hour."

He grinned ear to ear. "Yes mam. One hour."

She watched him turn and hurry back to his truck and drive toward the ranch bunkhouse. *Oh, Lord, help! My heart's in so much trouble and I'm too old for this.*

But she discovered, much to her delight, that there was nothing *old* about hanging out with AJ Call. She'd never been treated so special nor laughed so much in her life.

"How have you managed to stay single all these years? Seriously. I've never been lucky with my men choices. The good ones are always taken early in life. How'd you escape?"

His face pinked as he grinned. "Ah…I came close to a serious relationship a couple of times…but, I knew neither of those ladies were the right one for me."

She blinked and studied his sweet smile. "I wish I'd had just a little of that gift…to know when somebody's not the right one. I could have saved myself some misery." She paused and locked her eyes on his. "I'll bet you left a couple or more broken hearts behind you somewhere."

A large, strong hand reached across the table and covered hers while he studied her long, slender fingers and perfectly manicured pink nails—He rubbed and caressed each finger before glancing back up at her. "It's not exactly a gift that lets me know those things."

"So…are you a psychic?"

A smile brought twinkles to his eyes. He shook his head. "No, nothing like that."

He wasn't too sure at first how much he should try to explain to her, but then, if his faith in God Almighty was a turnoff to her or if she saw it as a joke, now would be the time to find that out. For him—that would be a surefire deal breaker as far as going any further with a relationship. He felt ashamed that he was hesitant to tell her how close he strived to live every day in a walking-talking relationship with his God. Many years ago, he had committed himself to Jesus Christ first—even if it cost him a long and lonely earthly life. And it seemed all these years like that was going to be the case. But regardless—he would not compromise that one thing.

"My faith in Jesus Christ is where I get my answers, Julie. The Bible tells us that the Holy Spirit—God's Spirit lives inside those who belong to Him and we are to allow Him to be our life's counselor. So, I talk to Him about...well...about everything and He counsels me about it."

She looked off into the space of the restaurant with narrowed eyes, then back at him. "I don't understand. I mean... He's my Savior, too, but...how does He tell you about things like who is the right person for you to be with?"

"The Lord speaks in a quiet voice inside of us. And it's like anything else—you have to learn how His Voice sounds and practice hearing it by listening for Him. And mostly I believe you have to *desire* to communicate with Him. *Really, truly* want that."

When her eyes began to tear, she grabbed her cloth napkin from her lap and dabbed at the spills on her cheeks while a nervous chuckle escaped. "Sorry about this. I've just never heard anything like that before. No church I ever went to taught about that."

He crossed his arms and leaned forward on the table. "I can't say that I learned that in church either, but what I *did* learn there, I believe it led me to taking the step of dedication that I took. I developed a true relationship with God by spending time during the night or early mornings at home in prayer and eventually...conversation. A relationship is two-sided. Both gets a chance to talk. I did that on my own many years ago just after my mother died. I'm telling you these things because I need you to know where I stand on that issue. Jesus Christ is first. Everyone else comes somewhere after that."

She wanted to ask, '*including me?*' And she wanted to ask if God spoke to him about her. But she didn't ask.

Instead she picked up the dessert menu and studied it. "Want to split a cheesecake with me?"

"I'd be honored, young lady."

He ordered one slice, two forks and two coffees.

A half hour later, AJ paid the bill and once they were back in the dually, he started the engine, then paused a moment. He wasn't sure how she felt about his stand on his Christian faith but figured that would show itself sooner or later. And probably *sooner.*

"I didn't mention this to you so if you'd prefer not to go—I can come back tomorrow. But, there's a man here in town who takes in stray dogs and tries to find homes for them. I thought I'd drop by his place and see if he's got a little somebody who wants to live on a ranch."

"I would love to go. That's exciting! Once I get settled again, I want to adopt a dog, too."

Hearing that was encouraging and a good sign of their compatibility, except for the part about getting settled again. That sounded like she still had plans to move on.

"He just lives a couple blocks around the corner."

"I visited a shelter for cats and dogs once. I don't know how you could make a decision when there's so many begging for your attention. I left there in tears."

He studied her profile while she solemnly stared straight ahead. "Were you thinking of adopting when you visited?"

The quick smile that usually spread her mouth didn't happen this time. In fact, he watched her struggle with an inner turmoil that he hadn't witnessed on her. It seemed he'd struck a nerve—a major one.

She cleared her throat, a catch breaking her voice when she answered. "No. I was looking for my…dog…Scout."

"Did he wander off from home?"

She shook her head slightly. "My husband kicked him and threw him out into the back yard. It was way below freezing. I ran out and got him, but…he jerked him out of my arms and left with him in the car. I never saw him again. I looked everywhere I could think of for months."

At that moment, AJ knew that the little dog hadn't been the only one who had suffered abuse at the hands of Julie's husband. *Julie's husband.* That was new and another matter for later. He gently reached out and wrapped his fingers around her upper arm, urging her to come closer. When she moved toward him, he grasped her beneath her leg and slid her all the way across the truck seat and low-set console and into his arms.

"Oh...now you're making me cry." She swiped at her wet face, but he just hugged her tighter against his chest and laid his cheek on the top of her head.

"I think someone else is responsible for these tears, baby girl, but I'm going to hold you until you cry all you need to."

At that, she relaxed her body against his and cried—and cried. Once she was spent, she raised up and pulled away from his tightly wrapped arms. Embarrassed and ashamed of her emotional break down, she scooted across the seat to her passenger side door and fished a Kleenex out of her purse that set on the floor of the truck.

"I'm so sorry, AJ. I can't believe I let myself do that. I've never been a crybaby."

He let her pull herself together before saying anything more. He knew there were a lot more tears left unshed. The smile she was attempting was a long way from reaching her eyes.

"Julie...don't ever be sorry for using the tears God supplied you. We all have to use them now and again. I would like to hear more about your Scout sometime." He reached out and lightly squeezed her shoulder. "Are you up to going with me to the shelter?"

Nodding her head vigorously, she managed a chuckle and a smile. "Yes. I would love to go with you."

"Good." He backed the dually out and headed further into downtown for only a block, then turned right onto a dark side street. In another block and a half, he pulled into the narrow driveway of an old, but one-story spread-out brick home that covered every foot of the half acre lot. The right side of the house had been added on to by a few hundred square feet and sided with something other than the original brick.

That add-on soon proved to be the well-kept area where up to twenty stray canines of every size and breed mixture was housed. Every wire pen was home to a four-legged furry pup. Some pens held as many as three.

The middle-aged woman with graying dark hair pinned on top of her head, that let them inside, had pointed them toward the kennels without any explanation. They walked through two long aisles of pens—most of the dogs were busy eating and didn't take notice of them. Except for one.

An older looking Golden Retriever mix lay on the cool concrete floor with its head resting between its front outstretched paws. Its eyes stared forlornly at AJ and Julie, stopping both in their tracks. Neither could move their eyes from the sad, depressed and underweight gaze that held them still.

Booted footsteps coming down the aisle behind them broke the spellbound exchange of communication between dog and man...and woman.

"Evenin', folks. Pick you out three or four. I'm about out of room."

"Hello. AJ Call and this is Julie."

"Ace Sandmann." He shook their hands and apologized for his being unwashed. "We just got through feeding and changing out a couple that didn't want to get along. What can I do for you today?"

AJ glanced around. "Looks like you've got your hands full here. We were hoping to find a pup that might like the looks of us."

"Well, most of them's got eyes that'll rip your heart out. That's why I've got 'em now." Ace laughed and shook his head. "You look familiar. Have we met?"

"In passing a few months ago at the Burger Gettin Place."

"Yeah, I remember. You work for the Double OO Ranch."

"Yes, sir."

Julie was quiet—still a little subdued after her crying spell, but she couldn't stop glancing back at the sad Golden.

"I see your wife is taken with my newest boarder."

Julie didn't care to correct the *wife* error and she noticed that AJ let it go by as well. Right now, her mind was on Scout—wondering if he had been dumped on the street—if he'd ended up in a cage like this and feeling abandoned by her. Maybe he wasn't even alive. She hated not knowing. But what she *did* know was this heartbroken little soul was going with her if he or she was for adoption.

AJ could see she was still in an emotional state and that she was also taken with the Golden pup. "What's the status on this one?" He nodded his head toward the Retriever.

"This is Sassy. Her owner brought her here—a lady who is moving into a nursing home in Jackson. She said she was sick and alone and couldn't take care of her. The lady cried when she left and," he pointed at Sassy, "she has refused to eat and just lays there depressed. I haven't been able to coax her out of it."

"How long has she been here?"

"Three days."

"Can you let her out?"

"I've tried, but she won't come out. She's grieving for her lady." Ace opened the door to the pen and called her, but she ignored him.

Julie went just inside and sat down on the floor. "Sassy girl, do you want to get out of this cage?"

The pup whimpered slightly and turned her gaze away from Julie. She didn't try to touch her, but continued to let her hear a gentle, soft voice.

"I know you miss your mom. But she got sick, Sassy. She can't take care of you now. So I'll take care of you for her. Maybe I can take you to visit her. Would you come with me and let me be your stand-in mom?"

Another tiny whimper.

She held out a hand, palm down, hoping she would at least turn her head toward her and sniff her.

Then suddenly, Sassy slowly raised up, got to her feet, walked to her and lay down in front of her, placing her chin on Julie's knee. Swallowing hard at the lump that suddenly formed in her throat, she stroked her head and gently rubbed a hand down her neck and thin little back.

The faint jingle of a collar and leash brought Sassy's head up. She stood up and practically walked into the leather piece that AJ brought in. Julie stood while he buckled on the red leather band and then handed the chain leash to her.

Julie's face lit up and she tilted her gaze up to his. "Are you taking her home?"

"*We* are."

The smile that jumped to her lips was the most genuine he'd seen on her—eyes sparkling like tiny diamonds.

She wasn't sure what *'we are'* meant. This was AJ's trip here to find him a dog. She couldn't help but feel that the sad and grieving pup needed her—or maybe she was just in love at first sight.

Ace picked up the pink blanket off the floor along with a brown, stuffed, floppy monkey. "These here came with her. She might feel more secure taking them to her new place. God bless ya'll." He rubbed Sassy's head. "See ya, girl."

Sassy moved a step closer to Julie until she was against her leg, then tilted her head to look up into her new lady's face. She smiled down at her and AJ watched the exchange with his heart about to burst. Julie needed this to happen. In fact, both girls needed this.

He shook Ace's hand, then followed the pair outside.

On the way back to the Double OO, after a quick drive-through for a hamburger for the hungry pup and dog food to take with her, Sassy sat on the console between her new people like she had been riding that spot all her life.

Julie glanced at AJ, waiting for him to say something concerning this dog and all he would do is meet her glance and smile.

A couple miles from the Luke's gate, he pulled the truck over onto a wide gated drive that led into another area of the ranch, put it in park and turned toward his passengers. "Ok, so I'll take this child of ours one month, you the next. Or......every other weekend for you...and..."

She burst out laughing. "You're nuts, you know that?"

He rocked his head back and forth and smirked his lips. "Yeah…I've been thinking that myself here lately. Seriously…do you need to make sure it's all right with Judd and Toni if you have this girl there? Or……I can, for the time being, take her on home with me until you get squared away with your plans."

Why that last statement—*squared away with your plans*—socked her in the stomach, she wasn't sure. It sounded so separated from him. It put a damper on the whole evening.

She nodded, "Yes, that would be best. I can let you know my plans and we'll go from there."

AJ heard the bland tone and after a few seconds, simply got back onto the highway and headed toward the Double OO ranch house.

***

CHAPTER NINE

AJ stirred in his sleep—There was no sound, but an intense stare bearing down on him, almost willing him to open his eyes. When he did, a smile, then a chuckle greeted his Sassy new friend and house guest. She was standing on her back legs, the front was reared up on his bed, a smile pulling both sides of her mouth.

"Well, if you're not a balm for this old cracked heart of mine, Miss Sassy girl." He stretched across the big bed and rubbed her front paws, then her nose. "I guess it's about breakfast time, huh?"

Her bark followed by a whiny whimper let him know she needed to go outside. He was quick at deciphering dog language after many years of practice.

He let her out the front door and stood with bare feet, sweats and short sleeved T on the cold porch to wait. Everything was new to her—including *him,* so he let her see him there until she completed her business and ran back to his side.

"Good girl, Sassy. Let's go inside and eat."

He was happy to see her so excited and secure with him but had no idea if she would remain with him for much longer. Julie had exited the truck in the Luke's back driveway without a word concerning her. She'd thanked him for a wonderful evening and kissed the dog on the nose and was gone. She was obviously upset, but he didn't believe it was about her memories of Scout. Her smile was big and—artificial, but the eyes always gave her away. She had different emotions showing in those green half-lidded pools—but mostly they were sad.

He'd hated to let her go like that, but Julie Langston had a lot of unsettled issues—a couple of them he knew about, some he could guess, but there were others he felt went too deep for her to talk about very easily. Even though he was more than willing to help her through all that, he couldn't force himself where she demanded her privacy.

But—he *did* have one ace he could play and ultimately help her win, with or without hands-on, so to speak, from him—God knew it all and he could pray.

With every heavy step she had taken to the back door, Julie desperately wanted to turn around and rush back into the dually and go home with AJ and Sassy. Her heart was breaking, but she couldn't figure out the exact reason. Why was she running—and what from? What had just happened?

Thankfully the house was quiet. A glance at the kitchen stove clock startled her. It was already nearly midnight, but then she remembered it was almost eight o'clock when AJ picked her up for a late supper. Over half their evening was spent getting acquainted with Sassy. Time—It was in high gear making her feel rushed and hurried and not knowing why about that either.

She locked the door behind herself and went upstairs to quickly change into pjs and curl up under covers in the darkened bedroom. Hot tears slipped down the side of her face and into her hair. She hated crying. For one thing, it created puffy bags under her eyes. Another thing was she'd done enough of that throughout her marriage to last the rest of her life. She wanted to laugh and feel happy and—be free.

Suddenly, she stopped crying and sat straight up in the bed. That was it! Her freedom was threatened. It had only been a short time since she'd been thankfully released from an imprisonment of fear and feeling like she was suffocating all the time. And she was about to jump right back in and slam the door on her—freedom.

At least she had discovered that she could still feel the giddiness of love, the desire for a man's strong arms around her. But hadn't she felt all that when she had first met Mark on the cruise ship. She stifled a groan, falling back onto her pillow and wrapped herself tighter in the bed covers as if to hide and protect herself.

"Sassy," she whispered into her pillow, then silently vowed to not think of her again. She knew what she had to do and the sooner the better before she lost herself all over again.

When she came downstairs the next morning, she was fully dressed for the day and carried her suitcase and makeup bag. Even though it was barely past eight, Toni was up and making coffee.

"Wow, girl, look at you! You *are* feeling better."

Toni turned around to respond, but her words died on her lips when she saw Julie prepared to leave. "What's all this?"

She dropped her bags and entered the kitchen. "Gotta go, girlfriend. I'm sure my welcome is getting on the thin side."

"It's no such thing. Jules…I'm just now able to really visit and…"

"Toni…I have to go. I'm sorry, but I've got a few more oats to sow before I die. I'm getting old. It's now or never."

"Sit down. I'll get coffee. There's bacon and scrambled eggs on the stove for you." Toni couldn't keep the disappointment out of her voice.

"No breakfast. Just coffee."

When they were both seated across the small dining table from each other, Toni grabbed a paper napkin and mopped at the escaping tears.

"Toni…"

"I'm fine, Jules. I'm just pregnant. So where are you going?"

She shook her head. "Not real sure. I just know it's time to go…somewhere."

"I thought you and AJ were hitting it off."

"Yes, well…we enjoyed each other. We're friends. He adopted a sweetheart golden retriever last night. Sassy. Her owner got sick and had to give her up." She didn't want to talk about AJ or Sassy, but she didn't have another subject, except— "I had the craziest dream last night."

Toni knew she was rambling out of nerves or an upset of some kind, but she felt a distinct urge in her spirit to give her space. "What was your dream about?"

She gazed off toward the wall as she tried to recall details. "Some of it is kind of fuzzy now, but I was getting off a plane and your mother-in-law, Maggie, was waiting for me. I was visiting her in Italy. I saw the town of Positano from her car. She was driving and I was taking in the sights. She turned to me and handed me something and smiled. I don't know what she handed me, but I eagerly took it. Then I woke up."

For a second, she was stunned, her mouth dropping open. "Jules...that's amazing!"

"It is? Why?"

"Because I had a phone call from Maggie last night. I mentioned you were here visiting and just road-tripping for a while. She invited you to come to Italy to visit her."

"Seriously?"

She nodded. "Yes. Her husband is on a business trip somewhere for a couple weeks. She sounded very serious and excited about it."

Julie looked like a light bulb had popped on behind her eyes. "Toni! Let's do this! We could fly out and ...oh, we'll have so much fun."

Toni was quiet a moment. "I can't go, Julie. I'm so tired from all the sickness and right this minute, I'm fighting a mild nausea. I think it would be too risky for me. But you should go. I believe *some* dreams are important to listen to—plus, you've been invited."

A growing sense of excitement had invaded Julie's veins. Disappointed that Toni couldn't go, but not enough to put a blight on her enthusiasm, she let Toni pull her from her chair and haul her into the ranch office. "Here—I'll get a call through to Maggie and you talk to her. Make plans and then we'll get a flight for you."

What in the world?" Granny Martha spotted the red-lettered sign printed on a rough-out slab of pine and hung prominently on the front of the chuck wagon—***Granny Martha—Sit a spell—Coffee up—***

Talk about it! "Don't have to ask who set me up in business. That girl has got me in more hot water since the day we met. Laura Lou Brandon, where are you?"

Laura and Daisy both peeped around the edge of the privacy fence gateway that surrounded the hot tub.

Martha spotted them after hearing the giggles on the wind. "There you are." She stomped her long, spindly legs up the small incline to where they were hiding. "Oh, I see now. You two are in cahoots. I knew there was a shenanigan going on. I felt it." She grabbed both women around their necks for a group hug and kissed each one on the cheek. "My day has been made, ladies. Thank you. Now, I better help Hank serve some breakfast." She headed back to the chuck wagon just as some of the Double OO crew pull in.

Judd, Toni and Jenny pulled up and parked alongside AJ, who just then, opened his truck door and stepped out. They watched him gently help a strange golden-haired dog out and ease it to the ground.

"Aww…look, AJ's got a new dog," Jenny squealed and piled out to be the first to pet it. "Does he bite, AJ?"

"She's a her and no, she loves attention. But let her smell your hand first and decide you're a friend. She's an *old* girl. Name's Sassy."

In less than a minute, Jenny had her arms wrapped around the furry neck, kissing her on the head and giggling at the returned wet-lick kiss on her face. It was Doggy Heaven for the pair, so AJ left them to enjoy each other.

"Morning AJ." Judd came around his truck and shook hands. "Looks like *Auntie* Jenny has taken up with a new-comer."

They both laughed and walked off toward the chow line.

Toni had headed for the pavilion, then turned around to see where her daughter went. "Jen, honey, don't get your school clothes dirty. Come get some breakfast before you have to leave."

"Yes, mam." She got up and headed for the chuck wagon with Sassy following on her heels.

A few minutes later, Jenny set her full plate on the table and sat down beside her mom—Judd set a plate in front of Toni and he and

AJ sat across from them. Sassy settled under the table close to familiar and friendly boots.

"AJ that's a beautiful dog. Julie mentioned, just before she left, that you had adopted her. She looks like she just needed somebody to love and take care of her."

AJ's face dropped before he could hold it still. *Before she left?* He grabbed his biscuit, looked down and fed a small piece to Sassy. "Yes mam, me and this girl seem to be bonding in a hurry."

Judd and Toni exchanged a split-second glance. Neither of them missed his reaction. He apparently had no idea she was going to leave.

"Although," he continued, "I don't think she's up to running with me all day. She'll probably wait for me in the bunkhouse—at least for now."

"I can babysit her at my house, please AJ?" Jenny stood up to gather her breakfast throw aways.

"Jenny! Come on—the bus is coming," Jesse, Jr yelled as he ran to his dad's dually for a ride to the ranch gate.

"Leave that, Jen. I'll clean it up," Toni said and waved her on.

"Thanks, Mom and I'll get Sassy from the bunkhouse after school. Okay? Okay? she yelled as she ran.

"Okay! Go!" Judd yelled and shook his head.

"Actually…" Toni crooned.

"Oh, here we go. I knew this was coming next." Judd playfully bumped the back of her head and laughed.

She ignored him as much as possible. "I'd love for Sassy to keep me company during the day while you're out—umm—until school's out, at least. Then, I'll have to share."

AJ smiled and nodded. "I'm sure she'll be a lot happier hanging out with you and Jen. But just know I can't guarantee that she doesn't have a bad habit or two—even though I haven't seen one, so far. She's been spayed, housebroke and loves attention—just getting up in age a bit."

"Sold! Drop her at the house on your way out."

"I will. Thank you."

Not a word was mentioned about Julie and Toni decided it was better left to the two of them. They were not kids that needed guidance. But it left an ache in her heart to see the hurt in AJ's eyes—The same pain Julie had left here with yesterday morning. Still—she believed her phone call from Maggie and Julie's dream, on the same night, had a God-driven purpose. It just didn't seem to bode well for AJ.

The sun was bright and the cold wind was more settled than usual, but AJ hadn't noticed. For the first time, he contemplated moving on from here—maybe retiring to work his own small ranch. He could build it up enough to make a decent living—or possibly sellout altogether and get a fresh start somewhere besides Wyoming.

He knew he was thinking out of the ache in his heart. But how much loneliness was a man required to take in this life? If he was being tested by his Heavenly Father—was it possible to even pass this test? He had walked away from two opportunities in his life to open his heart and world to a woman—to marry—have children. And both times, the Lord caused him to see red flags flying over both of them that would have given him grief that he didn't want to bring into his daily life. The Peace of God was the thing he sought for and cherished most. He lived with that Peace in his soul every day.

But not today.

He walked his ranch gelding toward the mountain range along the back side of the Double OO. He'd ridden every inch of this place over the years and he knew the tree-line on this end of the ranch was the one area he was more apt to be alone. Walking the edge of the pasture, he let his horse meander in and out of the tall pines at will.

Italy. She flew to Italy! How had she not mentioned something that huge? What on earth had he done—or said that made her pack up and leave the country?

Judd mentioned, while they were saddling up in the barn, that she had left the day before to visit Ms. Maggie. Afraid he might lose what little breakfast he'd just swallowed whole, he saddled and left abruptly. He'd lost his ability to take news in his usual stride.

How did he misjudge what he was feeling for her—or how *she* had responded to *him*—the kiss they shared. When he'd wrapped his arms around her and held her that morning in his bedroom and yesterday when she'd cried so hard over Scout. He poured these things through his mind over and over but couldn't come up with why she left like she did.

He wanted to pray. *God knows the answer to this*—but, he couldn't bring himself to do that right now. There was too much anger and confusion roiling inside him. It seemed that the appearance of Ms. Julie Langston had done nothing but up-end his entire world—stability—contentment, even his day to day life with his Lord. The only thing he could do now was work toward fixing himself.

He picked up the gelding's loose reins and headed toward the other side of the ranch at an easy lope. He had a commitment to foreman, Les Kane and Judd Luke. He knew they needed him on the job today. But—nothing felt the same, even being here on the Double OO. He had some serious decisions to make.

Julie had never been fond of flying and hadn't done much of it—but this particular flight from Cheyenne, Wyoming to Naples, Italy proved to be double the misery. The short flight from Jackson to Cheyenne was enjoyable enough, mainly because it was so quick—take off, eat a sandwich and land. But eleven hours on to Naples gave her too much time to worry about the plane being overloaded and falling out of the sky and feeling a heavy regret that she'd left without a word to AJ.

They had sort of adopted a dog together, or so she thought, but then, he'd said she should get on with her plans or something like that. It felt like a dismissal. Had she misunderstood him—jumped to a wrong conclusion? She didn't know what had actually happened, but a need to go was overwhelming by the next morning. *Not to Italy, though!* This seemed to come out of nowhere and suddenly—wham-bam and here she was on an eleven-hour flight out of the country. It was all because of a dream and a phone call—the combination that

Toni insisted was a directive from God. Wow! That now seemed a little woo-woo out there.

Well, the final analysis was that she was going to spend the next week or two in Positano, Italy. It was a little late to change this plan.

But—this was about preserving her freedom, making her own decisions without a man's demons and ego holding her in bondage—to any degree. That was unacceptable. Not for the remainder of her life would she allow that to happen to her again. This trip was exactly what she needed.

She lay her head back hoping to sleep a few hours. Instead, she relived every moment she'd spent with AJ Call—his beautiful smile, his laughter, his arms holding her while they shared a kiss that left them both breathless and laughing with joy. A picture of Sassy sitting between them on the console of AJ's dually formed in front of her. She drew her legs up and curled onto her side in the seat. With a hand covering her eyes—she wept.

Wow! Julie supposed this was what was meant by *Deja vu*. It was like she had been here before. She'd seen some of the details of this glorious picturesque little Italian village that seemed to fall off into the sea—She'd seen it in the dream.

Maggie was beautiful—model-style beautiful. She had to be in her eighties now but dressed in a gray and peach flowing ankle-length skirt with an ultra-light gray long blouse gathered and belted around her tiny waist. Her hair was pinned on top of her head—light brown with blondish tendrils loose around her face—a glowing, happy and youthful face.

"Hang on, honey," Maggie's laugh was delightful, "I've been driving these winding narrow streets for many years. I promise to get us home."

"Oh, I'm fine, Ms. Maggie. I trust you. I was just noticing how young and beautiful you look. I want to know everything you eat and drink."

She laughed gleefully and patted Julie on the knee. "It's called makeup mixed with a whole lot of happiness."

"Vitamins?"

More laughter. "Tons of them." She slowed and turned into a partially enclosed garage. "We're here. Let's get you settled into your room. I know you have to be jet-lagged. I have to go out to an appointment; and it's a few hours until supper, so feel free to nap if you want to."

They each grabbed a suitcase and the thin, feisty host led the way up a flight of stone steps that ended on a brick terrace, then into a cave-like opening with steps leading up and through an arched doorway into the most beautifully furnished den and kitchen combo apartment. The walls were white with white furniture as well as kitchen appliances and cabinets. Pillows and a mixture of area rugs and window shades threw in an array of colors in grays and blues and streaks of a rusty-red. It was Maggie all over the place. The high ceilings had exposed wood that was painted white and set into rock that appeared to be holding the house onto the side of the hill. Lots of smooth sanded wood pieces—a small bench, a collection of cutting boards hanging on the wall above a countertop in the kitchen, oversized driftwood candle holders at various heights filled in making for a comfortable down to earth feel. This villa was, by far, on her highest level of interior decorators' radar.

The guest bedroom was the same bright and cheerful abode on an upper split level above the kitchen with access to a terrace that overlooked a beautiful view of the beach and ocean. A bougainvillea canopy covered the terrace with an entrance to Maggie's master bedroom on the other end of the patio. Julie had never seen anything so beautiful and inviting—and *her* style.

Alone in her room, she sat on the edge of the bed and let herself fall back across the plush double bed comforter and closed her eyes. "Stunning," she whispered. "Pure bliss," and immediately an unsolicited picture formed in her mind of AJ—of him holding her and looking at her like he did that morning in his bedroom. If she'd ever seen a look of love in her life before—which she hadn't—that was it. And she'd packed and left *that* for a trip across the world. As beautiful as this place was—without that sweet love he was showing and offering to her— "Oh," she curled on her side and fought to swallow the lump before it wrecked her first day in—paradise.

"Julie."

She heard her name, but it took a minute to force herself to respond. Finally, she opened her eyes and sat up.

Maggie stood in the partially opened doorway looking as angelic as she had earlier with a smile to match. Her face looked like a light was shining on it—from somewhere. "Forgive me, honey. You've slept for three hours. I want you to be able to sleep tonight. There's an open market just down the street. Would you like to go with me to get fresh produce for supper?"

She stretched until her muscles screamed at her, broadening Maggie's smile. "Yes, I sure would. I'll be ready in five minutes."

The older woman closed the door and uttered a prayer of praise for Julie's life.

Ten minutes later, the stroll through the busy narrow street lifted Julie completely out of the somber mood she'd fallen asleep with. The market was a delight with every type of vegetable and meat, fish, fruit.

"I come almost daily for my evening meal. It's so healthy and fun to shop this way."

"I've never seen markets like this. Or, at least, I haven't been to one. This is so convenient to have it out your door. Just the atmosphere must make all this feel like you *live* on vacation."

"It does feel that way, Julie. I don't want to be anywhere else in this world but here. It's home."

A flicker of pain waved through Julie's eyes just then. Maggie saw it—but she had already discerned a sadness coming from her house guest.

The weather was unusually cool for September and after a delicious meal of vegetable salad, bread and wine, the pair retired to the upper terrace. Maggie touched a button on a remote to create an instant fire that flickered in the back wall of the deck. They sipped their wine in silence—enjoying the peace and tranquil world that shrouded them.

"So beautiful, Maggie."

Maggie stared at her for several seconds. "Yes, it is—except for who's missing? You weren't crying for *nobody.*"

Julie's eyes widened; her lips parted.

"I didn't eaves drop. You were crying in your sleep. Let's talk, sweetheart. It's just old Maggie here and I'm nearly dead so—you're relatively safe."

She smiled, then giggled. "You're so cute."

"Well, it's been a while since anybody called me *cute,* but I'll take it."

"AJ. His name is AJ.

"Call?"

"The same. He works…"

"For my son on the Double OO," Maggie finished for her. "A really nice young man. Is he still single?"

"Yes. He's never married. He told me he was waiting for God to send him the one He'd chosen for him. Does that sound crazy?"

"No. That sounds like AJ. Any woman who marries that man will have to have a strong commitment to God herself. He's one who certainly walks the walk, as they say."

Julie let her words sink in for a minute. She didn't know that much about AJ—hadn't spent enough time with him to *really* know him. "Kind of a fanatical Bible thumper?"

Maggie's laugh was a joyful sound. "Oh no—I wouldn't put that label on him at all. However, it has been a few years since I was in Wyoming and saw him."

"You seem to have known AJ really well."

"I lived on the ranch for a while before I met Conner Budly…in the old ranch house that I'd shared with Judd's dad. I got to know most of the hands—especially the ones who met in Judd and Toni's home for Cowboy Church. AJ Call was a young cowboy who was so obviously a man after God's own Heart. He had the sweetest and most humbled nature of anyone I've ever known." Maggie smiled at the way Julie was listening so intently—hanging onto her every word. There was no mistaking that her heart had AJ Call stamped right in the middle of it.

"May I be nosey and ask what is between you and him?"

"Nothing. Everything." She put her hand across her eyes, then waved it in the air. "Oh, lord, Maggie. I don't know how to answer that."

"Are you in love with him, Julie?"

She widened her eyes on the older woman, unable to find her voice for a minute. She didn't need to think about her answer, but was a little taken aback with the straightforward, to the point manner of this lady. She liked that. "Yes...I love AJ."

"I love him, too, but are you *in* love with him?"

"Yes, I am in love with AJ Call. But..."

Maggie reached for the iced-down bottle of wine and refilled both of their glasses. "Now...if you would like to talk about that *but,* I've got all night."

They both sipped their chilled white wine and sat quietly for a while, savoring the beauty of the evening.

Finally and very quietly, "I was...on a road trip...and stopped by Toni and Judd's ranch to visit for an hour or so. AJ came by at that time and we seemed to have an immediate attraction to each other. I ended up staying a few days to help Toni during her pregnancy sickness and AJ and I went out a few times." She took a sip of her drink—mainly to try and wash down the lump that wanted to form. "Then, we adopted a dog and I left the next morning...and here I am."

Maggie studied her emotional reaction to the mention of one man and a dog. That was too recent of an event for this kind of ardor. "So...is it AJ, the dog or something else you're about to cry over?"

"Oh, Maggie..." She rubbed her face with a trembling hand, then swiped at a spilled tear. "I miss both of them. I just can't seem to get anything right."

"What are you running from, honey? What are you afraid of?"

"I can't do it again."

"Do what, Julie?"

For the next several minutes, she told her the story of her two past marriages—relating details of her years with Mark and his horrendous control and physical abuse. She didn't get emotional, but spoke in a low, cold tone—a tone that Maggie understood.

"I haven't missed him. I wasn't sad that he was dead. That doesn't speak very well of my heart, does it?"

"You are very angry and rightly so. For all the years you were with him, *you* were rejected by him and in the worst way. In essence—he stole your identity. You couldn't be *Julie*—but had to be whoever he demanded that you be or he would hurt you."

"Why did I let that…that *freak show* do that to me? Why couldn't I leave?"

Maggie leaned toward her, reached out and covered her hand that was fisted in her lap. "Fear, sweetheart. Fear can be a powerful, immobilizing thing—as strong as a steel trap." She watched her struggle to hold her emotions at bay. "But I do have some good news for you. There's an upside to all this that has to do with why you came here suddenly—why you're sitting in that chair talking to me tonight."

She didn't say a word, but slowly raised her eyes to Maggie's and waited. A desperation rose up inside her—a compelling need to hear what this woman was going to tell her.

"You know I'm not one to beat around the bush and I'm not going to now. The fact is—Almighty God sent you here. He showed me in a dream about a week ago that you were coming to see me. I have a close relationship with Him, Julie, because I choose to be close with Him. He sent me here to live many years ago and uses Me to help the people who live here and many times—the tourists."

"You believe God sent me all the way here to talk to you about…my life?"

She nodded and sipped her wine. "I *know* He did. Oh, He could have used anyone right there on the ranch, but He's a fun God. He does His own thing. But, for sure, He had a purpose for doing it this way. After listening to your story, I see, in part, why He did. I lived through much the same thing you did—with Judd's father."

Surprise grew in Julie's eyes. "Did you hate him?"

"Yes, for a long time—until I met a lady who, long story short, introduced me to Jesus Christ and taught me how to overcome the hate and bad memories. Julie, do you know Jesus as your Savior?"

She nodded slowly, a little subdued at the path this conversation had taken. "Yes, I do. I was saved and baptized in a little church that I attended with Toni when we were in high school."

"I'm *so* glad to hear that." Her smile was alight in her eyes, showing a genuineness of her heartfelt words. "Now, I'm going to meddle a little more. Where have you been, spiritually, I mean, since then?"

Julie's gaze went into the dark night sky as her thoughts raced backward. Finally, she looked at Maggie almost blankly and shook her head. "I'm not sure what you mean. I attended church services here and there through the years, but...I mean...I know I have salvation. I don't know what else there is." She set her half full glass on the small table between their chairs. "If you are talking about the way AJ and...you... see things about God, I don't really understand *that*."

"I'm talking about studying the Bible and learning *about* the Lord, as well as, getting to know Him personally. Have you ever felt a desire to understand more about Him?"

She nodded. "Yes, now and then I've had questions pop into my mind about God."

That's why you were sent here...to me. Our Heavenly Father is ready for you to begin to grow in your spiritual life. You're His baby and He has taken care of you, like He did me...helped us out of messes we got ourselves in to. But eventually He calls us to grow up and He provides teachers to help us do that. You have to know within yourself that this is what God wants of you."

Both of them sat back and Maggie was quiet, letting her digest what she'd said to her.

***

CHAPTER TEN

By the time AJ stepped out of a steaming shower on the evening of his first day as a retiree from the Double OO—exhaustion kicked in without mercy. He didn't believe for a second that he'd worked any harder for himself than he did for Judd Luke or foreman, Les Kane. Why was he so tired?

It had been three weeks since he'd given Les his notice. It took that long for the workload to slow up and a new hire to come in. He'd refused to leave them in a lurch.

He and Sassy had gotten up this morning as usual, ate warmed over biscuits and gravy that Hank had bagged up for them the day before and hit the twenty-five-degree chilly air with gusto. The hay shed was enlarged over the past couple weeks during weekends and long night hours, then filled with good native grass hay. Unable to pass up a chance at a small herd of cow/calf pairs to purchase at a near giveaway price—he began his own operation. The heifers were guaranteed to add babies to his herd in the spring. He'd finished cross-fencing and repairing old fence, on the two hundred acres he had leased, to accommodate his new venture.

Dressed in black sweats, a long-sleeved gray T-shirt and thick gray socks, he padded into the kitchen to make sure Sassy's food and water bowls were filled. He'd brushed her off before they came inside as she generally made her way to the opposite side of his bed to sleep.

Normally he was famished about now, but not tonight. He was tired and a little achy. The past couple weeks seemed to have caught up with his fifty years. He could accept, easy enough, that he needed to slow the pace just a little. And right now, his big king bed was calling his name—loudly.

With doors locked and lights out, he and Sassy went upstairs and crashed. And once again, as with every single night since Julie had gone, he saw her smiling face, heard her laughter, her sobs over Scout—He could feel the touch of her wrapped in his arms. And somewhere in all that, he would fall asleep.

Tonight was no different, until he awakened suddenly, shaking with chills and dizzy when he tried to raise up. The lighted clock beside the bed read 2:33AM.

Sassy was sprawled on top of the quilt across his feet. Apparently, she'd already excused herself through her doggie door that he'd installed her first week here.

After a nauseating walk to the bathroom and back, he turned the electric fireplace up higher and slid under the quilts, shaking harder, his head throbbing. He couldn't remember the last time he'd been sick—but figured it would pass in a few hours.

Julie paid the attendant at the Jackson airport where her car had been stored for nearly a month—then serviced and made ready for her arrival early this morning.

After calling Toni and learning that AJ had retired and left the ranch, she couldn't help but feel as if she was responsible for that somehow. He had seemed so happy and contented in the work he was doing and had done for most of his life. She hadn't spoken to him since she'd left nearly a month ago. In such a short time, he had made a major change in his life. And in that same short time—so had she.

The past few weeks spent in Italy with Maggie was to say the least, a life altering experience. Not in her wildest imagination could she have made up the things Maggie had taught her—things about God and His Ways and Character. She knew she had a lifetime's worth yet to learn, but she knew He would help her become who He needed her to be—in His own time.

More than ever, she wanted to find AJ. He may not want to see her, but she had to apologize for how she'd treated him. And Sassy.

Did he still have her? Whatever she found—she would be okay. If he hurt her—sent her away—she would still be okay.

She headed in the direction of his home, hoping she could remember how to get there. Then she remembered that she could ask her Heavenly Father to help her find the right road. After requesting His help—she felt pressured to turn around. About a quarter of a mile back, she turned onto a narrow road without thinking. She just turned. It had been dark the one time she rode with AJ out here and now nothing was familiar. Just before she would have abandoned this way and turned around—she caught a glimpse of AJ's dually, then his sweet mountain styled log home.

Pulling in alongside his truck, a fist of nerves suddenly landed in the middle of her gut. She sucked a long, deep breath and exhaled slowly.

Scanning the area, she didn't see him or Sassy out anywhere—just a couple of horses standing at a round, metal pipe hay feeder. There were a few cows and babies grazing off a distance from the barn. She wondered fleetingly if they were all AJ's as she shut off the car motor, stepped out and let the door close.

A low growl warned her when she got about halfway between her car and the front porch of the house. She stopped and a loud barking ensued. Then she saw her—appearing to have come from the back of the house.

"Sassy? Remember me, girl?"

The dog approached her, still barking and Julie stood still, but put a handout, hoping she would catch her scent. When she finally did, she whined and her tail started swinging excitedly.

"Come here, baby. You know me, don't you."

The happy dog jumped up and landed dirty paws on her clean, pink hoodie, but Julie didn't care. She laughed and rubbed the dog's face and shoulders.

A sharp whinny from the pasture split her attention, then again when she noticed AJ coming out the front door and looking like something the cat had nearly finished off.

"Sass, get down." She immediately obeyed AJ and went to stand beside him. He stood on the porch looking at Julie as if he thought he was seeing an apparition.

She walked slowly toward him. "AJ?" He looked like he might pass out.

"I've...got to lay down," he mumbled as if it hurt him to speak.

Without hesitation, she rushed to him and wrapped her arm around his back—her other hand flat against his belly to steady him. "Come on...I'll help you to bed." She opened the door and then lay her hand back on his middle. "AJ, you're as hot as a jalapeno seed. Can you get upstairs?"

"Yeah. I have to put...hay out first." He tried to head toward the back door, but she pushed him around toward the stairs.

"I'll put out hay for you. Let's get you in bed."

Once upstairs, he lowered himself onto the bed and she covered him with quilts. Sassy appeared at the side of the bed and whimpered her concern.

"Come on, girl. Let's let him sleep," she whispered.

Downstairs Julie quickly scanned the open interior—dirty dishes and open bags of chips left on the table beside the recliner, muddy boots on the area rug in the den. The kitchen had smells that said bad trash can. The sink was full of unwashed pans and various dishes— Not like AJ.

This was so different from what she expected to happen when she pulled up at this house. She headed to the kitchen to look for a fever reducer med. Maybe a thermometer to see how high his fever was. Something for pain and fever was in a drawer under the silverware. She took that and a glass of water upstairs. He wasn't asleep—but moaning softly.

"AJ, sit up and take this. We need to get your fever down."

He raised up and swallowed two capsules, looking at her like he was confused.

"Julie," his voice was low and gravely, "why are you here?"

"Well, right now, to take care of you. I want you to drink more of this water. Just a few sips."

He drank a couple of swallows then laid back down.

"I think I need to get you to a doctor."

"No. Give pills time...to help."

She nodded reluctantly; not sure she was agreeing to the right thing. "I'm going out to hay your livestock. Are there any special instructions for feeding?"

"Check water," he grated.

"Are the cows in the far pasture yours."

"Yes."

"You rest. I'll take care of them." She turned and headed toward the door.

"Julie."

She stopped and turned completely back around toward him.

"Thank you for coming by."

She stared at him—wanting to say so many things, but this wasn't the right time. However, she needed to make him know that she would take care of everything while he was sick. "I'm not going anywhere, cowboy. I'll be right here."

Downstairs she grabbed his big overcoat hanging by the back door just as Sassy popped herself through the large doggie door. "Well aren't you special, Miss Sassy Call! You better come help me—make sure I do this right."

Looking out toward a fenced pasture far in the back of the acreage, white-faced red cows were lined up along the fence looking straight at her as she approached the barn. Both horses stood at attention and stared at her with their ears straight up. They seemed to realize she was not their person.

Bending over, she slid herself through a section of the white, paint-peeling pipe fence. That just seemed quicker than opening and shutting the gate. Both horses turned and trotted a few yards away before stopping and turning around again to stare at her.

"Hey...I'm a *good* guy. I just forgot to wear my white hat." They didn't seem amused.

She realized immediately that she had to go to the opposite side of the barn to get to the hay. Crawling back through the fence rails, she went around and pulled a square bale off the stack. Half carrying and half dragging—she finally got it through the gate and up to their hay feeder. After a little rough pushing and pulling, she loosed the bale from the string it was tied with and tossed a couple blocks at a time into the bin. At least she remembered how to do this from her childhood years with Toni and her Uncle John Baxter's ranch in Texas. Funny how some things come back to you after long years away from it. It almost felt like the most natural thing in the world to bust up a hay bale and feed horses.

Okay—so on to the next part. The cows. Hmm. That was a long way to drag ever bit of an eighty-pound bale of hay. There should be a wheelbarrow around here.

Before she could look for it, the unmistakable sound of a diesel truck came around the house and pulled up alongside of the barn where the hay was stacked. It was AJ's dually and AJ stepped out of the driver's side door. He was wearing a sweatshirt for a coat, being as she had borrowed his heavy coat and gloves.

By the time she reached the truck, he had already thrown five bales into the bed. He wore another pair of leather gloves, but she could see his hands and arms were trembling.

"Let me finish this. You need to be in bed."

"Get in," he responded, his voice was gentle, but still hoarse.

When she started around to the passenger door, he motioned to her. "You drive."

She scrambled in behind the wheel and he stood up on the step-side at her window. Drive to the fence down there. I'll throw these bales over the fence."

She didn't waste time, but hurried, concerned that he was going to be sicker after stirring around and out in this cold.

Back at the barn, he easily tossed two more bales into the horse's feeder, ripping the tight string around them in one easy motion. He threw the strings into the back of the truck, then checked the water level in their large round galvanized trough.

Half full was apparently good for now. She made a mental note to keep a watch on that.

By the time he drove them back to the side of the house, his eyes were showing a deepening pain and misery.

"AJ, do you need to go see a doctor? I can take you to the hospital ER."

"I'm sure it's a flu bug. I'll be all right in a day or so."

"I could have finished feeding. You didn't have to come out."

He gazed out the windshield for a few seconds, then turned to her. "I watched you wrestle that hay bale to the horse feeder. Now that you know the easiest way…" He pulled the keys from the ignition and handed them to her. "Take a knife with you to cut the string next time." He opened his door to step out but went to his knees on the hard ground.

"Oh, Lord, help!" She scrambled across the seat, stepped to the ground beside him and slid his big overcoat off of herself. Wrapping it around his shoulders, she squatted down beside him, holding it tight around him. "AJ, I'm going to take you to the hospital."

"No! No. Give me a minute. I'll get back to bed for a while."

Once she helped him up and back up the stairs to bed—she had decided to find the nearest town for some over-the-counter flu meds, juice and good soups. He felt a little cooler to her touch, so that was good.

Just as she headed out the door, Sassy came around the house whining and seemingly wanting something from her. "What's the matter, Sassy? I'll be back. You stay with AJ and keep him in bed 'til I get back. Okay?"

She barked and half turned to look toward the back of the house, then whined and barked again before running around the side of the house again.

Curious—Julie walked quickly that direction, figuring she'd gone inside through her doggie door to find AJ. Instead—she found a couple of visitors standing side by side just off the back porch and looking at her with pitiful, hungry eyes. Two furry, very thin pups. Her heart broke at the sight of their skin and bones bodies—and eyes begging for help. Even Sassy was campaigning on their behalf.

Julie turned back to the front of the house and went inside to find something to feed them. She emptied the small amount left in Sassy's dog food bag and carried it out in a tall tea glass—all she could find at the moment. She poured each a portion out on the grass a little distance from each other and watched them eagerly devour it. She rushed back inside for a bowl of water and set it down on the edge of the porch as she headed on to her car to get what she needed for AJ. She made a mental note to add a large bag of dog chow to the list.

As soon as she reached a higher elevation, her cell received a signal, so she pulled over and called Toni.

"Hey, Jules—I've tried to call you a couple of times. Where are you?"

"That's what I need to ask you."

"You're lost!?"

"Well, I've been at AJ's. Toni he's really sick with the flu or something like it. He won't go to the doctor or the ER, so I'm needing to buy something for him to take. I don't know where I am or where a town is from here."

"Which way did you turn on the highway?"

"Right."

"Okay, good—keep going and you'll come to a sign showing two or three small towns. Go to Frontier. It has a supermarket and a pharmacy and gas station."

"Wonderful, thanks!"

"Will you be staying there?"

"Yes, I will. He needs my help. He's very sick. Pray for him, Toni."

"Absolutely—Judd and I will pray together. Call us if you need our help."

"I will."

She hung up and hurriedly got to town and loaded up.

Twenty minutes later, she pulled into AJ's drive and was greeted by two wagging little tails. Sassy wasn't with them.

"You poor little souls. I'll get you fixed up in a bit. Right now, I've got a very sick man on my hands." She was talking as she unloaded the car.

After opening a carton of an organic chicken soup from the grocery store's deli and readied it to heat up on the stove, she fixed a hot lemony drink that was supposed to help ease flu symptoms and took it upstairs.

He opened his eyes as soon as she entered the bedroom. Sassy sleepily lifted her head from the foot of the bed, making Julie smile.

"How are you feeling?"

"Rough."

"This is supposed to help those *rough* symptoms. See if you can get it down and I have chicken soup ready to heat when you want it."

"Thank you. Leave it here. I'll sip on it. Can't move my head right now without getting dizzy. How long will you be here?"

She knew what he was asking. *For the rest of my life,* she wanted to say. "As long as you need me to be," she said.

"Thank you." He closed his eyes and she went downstairs.

There were so many things running through her mind at this moment. Her brain was in multitask mode and she knew she needed to slow the thoughts down and organize it all.

Peeking out the back door, she saw the two strange pups curled up together asleep. One was a medium sized, brown lab mix and its sidekick was sort of Scotty looking—gray with white markings on its head and feet—much smaller than its companion. They were most likely dumped or had been lost for a long time—nearly starved and in need of baths.

AJ was not ready to eat and the dogs were satisfied and sleeping, so—she glanced around the open interior of the house and decided her next move would be to clean house. This mess didn't look like AJ. The thought crossed her mind that if he'd missed her even half as bad as she did him when she was in Italy—and he, not knowing that she was truly in love with him—maybe he just didn't care much how he kept his house. She almost hoped that was the case.

With him—it was hard to tell if he was angry with her. He was always so level calm and reasonable.

Over an hour later, the house was back in good order. As she was about to head up to check on AJ, a diesel engine whined into the front drive.

A man and woman, looking vaguely familiar to Julie, got out. She stepped out on the front porch.

"Hi—Julie Langston?"

"That's me."

"I'm Daisy Cory. This is my husband, Mitch."

They exchanged handshakes.

"Mitch works for Jesse Brandon at High Point Dude Ranch."

"Oh, of course. I thought you looked a little familiar. I would invite you in, but AJ is not feeling well. He's sleeping."

"That's why we're here." Mitch said. "Toni Luke called me and asked me to check on him. I know AJ's got some medical training, but I've got more—a little more pull for getting him an antibiotic if he needs it."

"Oh—thank the Lord." She opened the door and Mitch and Daisy were greeted by a happy, tail wagging Sassy, who jumped and twisted around like a young pup.

The couple both laughed and called her by name. "We missed you too, Sassy girl," Daisy squeaked at her.

Julie realized then that AJ had been taking her to work with him and had made herself a few friends.

"Just head up those stairs, all the way." Sassy followed him.

"Do you and Mitch drink coffee, Daisy."

"Yes, that sounds good."

"I'm so amazed at this. Mitch is a direct answer to my prayer for AJ. He wouldn't let me take him to the hospital."

Just then, a little gray Scottie head poked through the doggie door and stared with huge sunken eyes as if waiting for an invitation to come in.

Julie squatted down and smooched to her or him to come on in. Cautiously and slowly the pup came to her where Julie immediately began to rub and pet it. "You're okay, little one. Nobody's going to hurt you here."

"Aww—how sweet. Is she yours?"

"No—well, I don't know," she chuckled. "This one and a friend showed up this morning from the back field. They're both starved. I fed them a little that Sassy had left and bought a bigger bag of chow this morning. So—she's a she?"

"Yes. I noticed when she stepped through the little door."

Julie opened the back door to find the brown dog sitting there looking lost. When she stepped out to pet it, it flopped over on to its side, one back leg up in the air. Girl! She pat her nose and rubbed behind a matted, dirty ear.

Daisy was making fast friends with the little Scotty in the kitchen when Mitch came down the stairs. "Do I smell coffee brewing?"

At the sound of the deep male voice, the Scotty practically flew through the little door and both furry girls ran toward the barn like their lives depended on it.

"Oh gosh, what happened?" Daisy looked shocked.

But Julie got it. Sadly, she could identify with the pup's fear. She stepped back inside and attempted to get coffee cups filled. "I think it was Mitch's voice. Apparently, they have been traumatized by a low gruff voice—a man's voice probably."

Mitch stopped part of the way into the kitchen and looked from one to the other, confusion creasing his brow. "What did I do? I'm innocent, I tell ya!"

Julie laughed. "Yes, you are. I have two stray dogs that were just here, but your voice, I guess, made them run for cover. That's actually good to know about them."

"What if they run off and don't come back," Daisy fretted.

"I feel sure they'll be back for more food. Those poor pups are too hungry to run far from a food bowl."

She handed a cup of coffee to Mitch. "How's AJ?"

"Thank you, mam. He's got a bad head cold and I'd say bronchitis. The stubborn old coot won't let me do any more for him, but I'm going to get him a round of antibiotics and bring them right back out." He slurped a sip of the hot coffee. "Hmm—this sure hit my spot. Thanks again."

"You're more than welcome, Mitch. And thank *you.*"

"Daisy, if you'd like to stay and visit while he gets the meds for AJ, I'd love the company."

"Thank you, yes I'd love that. Maybe we could go find the pups."

"I was just thinking that. I'm going to take a mug of soup up to AJ first."

Mitch left and Julie went upstairs.

AJ was partially propped up with pillows behind him, his eyelids puffy and lips feverishly red. He gave her a half smile as she entered the room that made her spirit want to sing.

"I'm not even going to ask you how you're feeling—so, how about I help you get some of this soup down." She glanced at the lemon drink she'd left earlier. The glass was empty.

"Do I look that bad," he growled through his raw throat.

"Worse. So, you better slide this soup down that throat."

He couldn't hold back the laughter that bubbled up—but made him cough painfully. "*That* bad and you're still here?"

"Yeah, well, if I catch this mess from you—you're going to be looking at *my* ugly until I'm well."

He reached for the soup. "That I will, mam, and it will be my pleasure."

She looked at him—almost not believing *anybody* on earth could be this congenial under all circumstances. "I wasn't sure you would want to see me again after the way I left."

He gazed into her eyes a few seconds. "I had my moments. So…why did you come back—Come here?"

"To apologize for running out like I did. I have no explanation for the abrupt way I did it, but God sent me there…to visit with Maggie for a few weeks."

His hand shook as he handed her the soup. He'd drank half of it.

"I'd better let you rest."

"Julie…I'm glad you're here." He closed his eyes and was asleep before she could force herself to move her gaze from his face and leave the room, brushing away a couple of wet drops from her cheeks.

Both women finished off their coffee, then headed to the barn.

"I picked up a little dog that had been dumped and then realized she'd had puppies recently." Daisy told Julie the story of the mama dog and her babies.

"Oh, that's such a sweet story—at least the ending is. I can't, for the life of me, understand how anyone could leave a helpless little animal in the middle of nowhere to starve."

"Ever since I was a little girl," Daisy said, "I've thought of owning a place where I could take in unwanted dogs and cats—like an adoption center for them. I visited a place like that on an elementary school field trip and it stuck with me all these years."

"Did you mention that idea to Mitch?"

"Yes, but as long as we live on High Point ranch, it's not an option. The liability is too high bringing strays in, particularly with so many kids on the ranch."

The idea was intriguing to Julie, especially after witnessing so many sad pups that were caged at Ace's facility in Jackson Hole. These little needy critters seem to be too plentiful.

"There they are Julie." Daisy pointed to the noses poking out from behind a hay bale in the furthest corner of the barn.

"Come here, you two," Julie called to them, but they crouched further into the corner. Both were shaking in fear. "Okay…let's just bring their food and water down here."

The wheels were spinning in Julie's head as they walked back in the house from making a warm, safe place in the hay for the pups. They had promptly devoured the dog chow and curled together on their blanket that Julie retrieved from her car.

She figured she had two options. If AJ was agreeable, she could build a facility here on a small section of his property for a small animal shelter. If that didn't work out—and there were several things that could go wrong with that—she could easily purchase land somewhere in this area herself. She'd need help and possibly Daisy would be interested.

Scout's House.

When that name suddenly popped into her mind, tears sprang up with it. Her heartbeat even picked up speed. Somehow, she knew God had just placed His stamp of approval on the idea. This was her calling—from her Father. She wanted to jump and shout but held herself together so not to disturb AJ or label herself as an idiot in front of her new friends. There were a few things to be worked out before she was ready to announce this to anyone—anyone except AJ, that is.

It was five days later when AJ finally felt strong enough to get up and come downstairs. "I don't know what you're cooking, but I want some."

"It's my famous beef stew. I fixed you a place in front of the fire. Get comfortable and we'll eat in there."

"Woman, I'm going to owe you for the rest of my days."

She watched him move slowly to his easy chair. He'd put on the fresh sweats and T-shirt she'd laid out for him and thick socks that were more like slippers. His hair was wet from the shower and he was clean shaved. If she'd ever seen a *beautiful* man in her life—he was it—from the outside to his deepest soul inside.

"Yes, you are. Every day of it!" She set his bowl of stew and crackers on the table beside his chair, then went to get hers.

Afterward, she sat on the floor closer to the fire and next to Sassy who had curled up to nap.

AJ thought the scene he was witnessing in his den tonight was all a man could ever dream up—a beautiful woman who had cared for him while he was sick, made the best home cooked food he'd ever had in his life and taken care of his horses and cattle single handedly, plus bathed and cared for two stray pups, including hauling them both to a veterinarian to be checked out and vaccinated—all in the space of a week.

But those were not the best and most important things. There was one more—The way she looked at him—the purest of love that he saw, like a little blazing fire deep in her eyes every time she gazed into his. He hadn't seen this light in her before her trip to Italy. But he recognized it. It was the love light of the Holy Spirit of God. What had happened to her during the weeks she was gone?

He scooted forward, then slid off his chair to the floor and reached for her arm to pull her closer to him. Using the front of the recliner bottom for a back rest, she snuggled against his side and felt his arm wrap around her. Squeezing her tighter, she involuntarily sighed heavily and laid her head on his shoulder.

God, let him be mine forever.

Lord, let her be the one.

He kissed her forehead and rested his head against hers. "I was just curious—when exactly should I begin this payback that's going to take the rest of my life? Do I need to be a *perfect* man first?"

She raised up and looked him in the eyes. "You couldn't be any more perfect if you worked hard at it. I know I'm far from a perfect woman, but…I *can* be a *better* woman than you knew, even a few weeks ago."

When her eyes filled and spilled over, he brushed a thumb over the wet. I would really like to hear what happened while you were gone."

She brushed her damp face with both hands, pushing loose strands of hair back at the same time. "And I need to tell you."

She told him about the dream she'd had the night they adopted Sassy and about Toni's phone call from Maggie the same night. "I felt so compelled to leave immediately…but, I didn't know where to until Toni told me Maggie invited me to come to Italy. I *had* to go. *Now* I realize God was moving me and leading me there. Maggie told me that the Lord God had told her I would be coming and what He needed her to do when I got there." She saw his eyes grow at that.

"Wow!"

"I won't go through a months' worth of details, but she taught me about the ways of God. For instance—how to forgive someone like Mark who I felt such hatred for, even after his death. I don't feel love for him, but I'm beginning to feel less of an aversion to the memories now when he comes to mind. It's a process and much less of a struggle to do now than when I began. She said the Lord would change me on the inside after a while. I just have to continue fighting the good fight of faith for it until then."

They were both silent for a while.

"There's one more thing I need to tell you. I don't know how you feel about it, but it's who I am now...so you have to know. Maggie prayed over me many times, but once, she prayed for me to receive more of God's Spirit on the inside of me...to give me a prayer language that the Bible calls *other tongues.* A few nights after that prayer, I woke up in the middle of the night...about 3AM..." she started to giggle and slapped her hand over her mouth, "jabbering..." she laughed harder, "like...like a mag...pie! Oh my Lord! That...was the funniest thing."

She just realized that AJ had his hand over his face trying to stifle his laughter, but to no avail. They laughed in each other's arms until both their faces were wet.

When they both sat up straighter and wiped their faces, AJ managed to finally speak.

"I'm laughing, baby, because the same thing happened to me one day out in the pasture while I was swimming in a livestock watering tank. It was years ago, but I'll never forget a second of it. I got so happy I thought I was going to drown."

"God can be a real riot sometimes," Julie said.

"That He can. I got God-stories that would kink your beautiful hair. But..." he turned toward her and cupped her face in his large, warm palms, "there is one thing you got wrong and I need to clear it up for you."

"O...kay."

"While you were gone, I prayed a lot, *for* and *about,* you...and our Father God informed me that I should be patient because He was preparing the *Perfect* woman for me. You *might* be better, but *for sure,* perfect. And that came straight from the Top."

She laid her hands on top of his and the intensity of their feelings washed over them again and again as they kissed—each knowing for certain that—*he was hers* and *she was the one.*

Later as they sat holding each other and enjoying the firelight dancing around the darkened room—AJ simply whispered, "Julie, will you marry me?"

She simply whispered back, "Yes, I will."

"Oh…my life is *so* made."

She chuckled. "Well aren't we a couple of twinkies. Mine is too!"

"We should plan our wedding…like tonight!"

She thought about that. "Honestly, AJ, I don't care about a wedding. I've been there. What do you want?"

He mulled the idea over for a full minute. "Truth?"

"Truth."

"I want to see my bride in a white wedding dress. I want the world to see the prize God gave this old cowboy. I've waited an awful long time for you."

She smiled up into his face, barely able to believe the joy this man brought to her soul. That wouldn't be her choice, but she realized he'd never been married. So—this was his time to shine and she would do all in her power to make it happen for him. "We better get to planning."

Judd Luke stood directly in front of the podium—Best Man, Grandpa Hank, stood beside AJ. The pews were filled with cowboys from both ranches, all the ranch families and many others from the Cowboy Church congregation. But—they all faded from AJ's sight when the first organ notes of the Bridal March sounded and the most beautiful thing he'd ever seen in his life suddenly filled the doorway at the opposite end of the sanctuary. His eyes drank in the length of her white satin, floor length, fitted wedding gown. His gaze traveled back up to the bouquet of tiny pink roses surrounded by white baby's breath—then, up to her face. She was looking at him, her eyes glittering as she walked so slowly alone—no one giving her to him except the Lord God who had brought them together.

Even the awes and quiet chuckles didn't break their locked gaze from each other, when the congregation saw Toni Luke helping Sassy carry Julie's dress train that was attached to her own white satin collar and wrapped in the same flower arrangement as the bridal bouquet.

By the time Julie reached the front, AJ stepped to her side and with a trembling hand, took hold of hers. Judd started to speak, but his words were arrested by the lump that formed in his throat at the sight of AJ's tears running down his cheeks.

As if on cue—Best Man, Hank, rubbed and swiped his eyes and set off several of the cowboys who had known and worked with AJ for a long time. Each felt there wasn't a more deserving man among them to have the kind of happiness their *brother at heart* was finally experiencing.

With all the sniffling and face swiping going on—Granny Martha thought she'd better step in and do a little damage control. She stepped away from her seat and announced, "Okay—let's dry it up, because if this bride starts bawling and ruins that fancy make up, we'll never hear the end of it."

The whole place broke up laughing and Pastor Judd managed to get on with the ceremony.

When they were finally pronounced husband and wife—AJ pulled his bride into his arms, making a deliberate show of positioning her just right, slightly bent backward and then, kissed her like the starving man that he was—sharing their *loved* and *in love* joy before God and man. Julie's giggling brought the house down with laughter and hoots.

Granny Martha laughed, then teared up. "Well, they just *had* to get *me* bawling."

****

EPILOGUE

Five months later

AJ strode through the front doorway of the house so excited he was close to popping the snaps on his 8-Bar western shirt that Julie had gotten him for their first Christmas. "Okay…you can go out back now," he said to Julie, with as much nonchalant cool as he could hold himself to.

"Should I peep out the door first? Is it alive?"

He laughed. "Nope. Just run right out there. I promise it won't bite."

Maggie had no idea what AJ was trying to surprise his wife with, but she didn't want to miss it. She picked the perfect day to visit their home before she would fly back to Italy tomorrow—to her easy does it, laid-back life. She didn't remember so much hustle and bustle, circus type atmosphere when she lived here so long ago. She followed AJ out—both of them watching Julie.

And she saw it before she got all the way down the back-porch steps. She stopped in her tracks on the bottom step—her eyes rounded as her hand slowly came up to cover her open mouth. Tears immediately flooded her eyes and spilled onto her hand.

"Oh…oh…"

AJ stepped down behind her and wrapped his arms around her. He pulled her tight against him and pressed the side of his face against hers. "Like it?"

"Yes…but…how did you know?" She knew she had never mentioned to a soul—not even to him—about that name. But there it was—a huge sign over the door of their newly built animal shelter—SCOUT'S HOUSE.

"I dreamed it," he said. "Literally—I saw this building and that name on it a few days after you asked me to consider this project. You remember, I wasn't sold on the idea at all, but then I was shown this in a dream and I knew God's Hand was on it."

She swiped at her tears. "He said that name to me months ago when the idea first came to my mind. But I never mentioned it…and…look at that!"

Maggie stepped down and hugged them both. "Isn't God just the greatest at surprises?"

Julie hugged Maggie. "I'm so glad you were here. And," she looked up at AJ, "thank you, honey. I'm so overwhelmed at this."

AJ patted both women on their shoulders." How about I get the grill fired up and we celebrate with a T-bone."

Julie nodded, still swiping at her damp cheeks. "Thanks, babe. The salad is ready, so I'll show Maggie our wedding pictures while we're waiting."

They settled at the kitchen bar with the album.

"I hated that I couldn't come for the wedding. Toni and Judd are still talking about that one."

Julie chuckled. "Sometimes we still laugh and talk about it, too. AJ cried when he saw me in my wedding dress—then, all the cowboys in the place were crying, even his best man, Hank Walton. I think he cried the hardest."

Maggie was laughing and crying at the same time, listening to Julie's rendition of the ceremony.

"*And*…of course, Granny Martha stepped out and told everybody to *dry it up because if this bride starts bawling and ruins that makeup, we'll never hear the end of it.* The whole place broke up laughing and finally Judd got to the vows."

"And I missed all this! What a beautiful and fun memory for the two of you."

"I bought this beautiful cake and AJ found a great country music band. We danced in the pavilion for hours like nobody was watching. Oh—and I had all the ranch cowboys to wear their old jeans, boots *and* spurs. I think I heard all that jangling metal for a week afterwards," she chuckled. "AJ loved it."

The photos were telling the same story as Julie, but her flamboyant description brought them all alive.

"Soup's on, ladies," AJ announced as he carried in a platter of juicy, sizzling steaks.

After supper, they walked Maggie out to her rented car. "Kids, this has been such a joy. Thank you for letting me share today with you. And being here for my brand-new grandson's delivery last week was over the top. John Baxter Luke. Judd and Toni and Jenny are on cloud nine—maybe ten! And they're having a second grandson just any day. I think my little villa in Positano is going to seem sadly quiet when I get back."

After an exchange of hugs, she drove away.

Standing in the front yard, AJ and Julie held each other, rocking back and forth.

"Oh, I nearly forgot." AJ glanced toward the house. "There's a message on the phone from Hank. It seems Kaitlyn Kane went in for a checkup this morning and she had to be taken for an emergency C-section. Everybody's fine. They have a healthy baby girl."

"That's wonderful. Sounds like all is well in our neck of the world today."

He pulled her back into his arms and kissed her like a wild man, making her squeal. Just then, Sassy and their other adoptee—little Scottie girl came racing around the corner of the house and broke into their moment with serious requests for attention. AJ laughed at their competitive insistence for a rub on the head. "Speaking of our neck of the world."